CW00458138

323

The relationship between Kerry and her stepbrother Ross had always been a kind of unarmed combat, and it didn't help at all when her stepfather died and left all his property, and the family business, equally between them. The obvious answer to it all was for them to marry—but how could she, when she didn't even like Ross? And that was before Kerry found out about Margot Kilkerry!

Books you will enjoy
by KAY THORPE

THIS SIDE OF PARADISE

From the start, Gina and her so-called friend Marie were at cross-purposes about their luxury holiday in the Bahamas. Marie was after a man—with or without marriage, if he was rich enough, Gina just wanted a once-in-a-lifetime holiday. But she couldn't really blame Ryan Barras when he got entirely the wrong idea about her. Why did it matter so much what he thought of her, though?

THE MAN FROM TRIPOLI

For reasons that seemed good at the time, Lisa had married Bryn Venner and gone out to live in Libya with him. She knew he didn't love her, and she thought she had no feelings for him—until, belatedly, she realised that she had fallen in love with him. Which was not the best time to find out about his liaison with Andrea Farron . . .

BITTER ALLIANCE

Liam Caine had had no opinion of Jaime from the start—but that didn't prevent her feeling wildly attracted to him, and when he suggested that she pose as his fiancée Jaime found herself agreeing. Could she go even further and marry him—knowing that he would still never trust her, let alone love her?

FULL CIRCLE

Five years had passed since Sara and Steven Masters had separated, and now she had come to meet him in Florida to ask for a divorce. But instead they became reconciled. The wheel had come full circle—but didn't it seem more likely that it would come full circle in every way, and that yet again they would find themselves unable to live together?

THE DIVIDING LINE

BY

KAY THORPE

MILLS & BOON LIMITED
17–19 FOLEY STREET
LONDON W1A 1DR

All the characters in this book have no existence outside the imagination of the Author, and have no relation whatsoever to anyone bearing the same name or names. They are not even distantly inspired by any individual known or unknown to the Author, and all the incidents are pure invention.

The text of this publication or any part thereof may not be reproduced or transmitted in any form or by any means, electronic or mechanical, including photocopying, recording, storage in an information retrieval system, or otherwise, without the written permission of the publisher.

This book is sold subject to the condition that it shall not, by way of trade or otherwise, be lent, resold, hired out or otherwise circulated without the prior consent of the publisher in any form of binding or cover other than that in which it is published and without a similar condition including this condition being imposed on the subsequent purchaser.

First published 1979
Australian copyright 1980
Philippine copyright 1980
This edition 1980

© Kay Thorpe 1979

ISBN 0 263 73195 2

Set in Linotype Plantin 10 on 11½ pt.

Made and printed in Great Britain by
Richard Clay (The Chaucer Press), Ltd., Bungay, Suffolk

CHAPTER ONE

'YOUR stepfather was a fine man, Miss Rendal,' intoned the vicar, holding out a kindly commiserating hand. 'We shall all miss him.'

None so much as she, thought Kerry, moving on and out of the small chapel into the welcoming brightness of the late September sunshine. Yet she refused to let sadness take over completely. Andrew Sinclair had gone the way he would have wanted to go; swiftly, without lingering illness. At sixty-nine years of age his life had hardly been spent, but there was comfort in the knowledge that he had enjoyed what he had known of it in his own way and no one else's.

Ross Sinclair was somewhere behind her. She had seen him waiting outside the crematorium chapel when the cortège had arrived. One would have thought he could at least have had the common decency to come to the house first. Death surely cancelled all family differences, no matter how bitter.

Even after six years she had known him immediately: the same crisp dark hair surmounting a face which was a younger replica of his father's. Strong-willed the two of them, and it showed in Ross the same way it had showed in Andrew, hardening the line of the jaw and forming a mouth capable of changing from mobile humour to rigid implacability in the space of a moment. If the word compromise had figured in either man's vocabulary the split would never have happened in the first place. Andrew had missed his only son, she knew, but would never have admitted it to her, or to anyone else. One could only hope that his own particular stubbornness had not extended beyond the grave, although with the law as it stood no total disinheritance would stand up in court anyway, and Andrew would have known that.

No, Ross was safe enough. The business which had been the cause of his leaving both home and country would now be his to do with as he wished. Six years in the States would hardly have reversed his ideas: the hard sell was born over there. No doubt he would waste little time in reorganising Sinclairs into featureless conformity, tossing away almost a hundred years of retail history as if it meant nothing.

Sinclairs Department Store had its foundations in a tiny draper's shop founded in the late eighteen-hundreds by Andrew Sinclair's grandfather Henry. From such relatively humble beginnings had grown the present four-storeyed emporium boasting no fewer than twenty-seven separate departments and employing a considerable staff. Sinclairs was not just the finest store in Medfield, it was the only one of its kind. Various chains held monopolies on certain items, but only in Sinclairs could the shopper buy everything and anything from a needle and thread to a costly three-piece suite without moving more than a few feet up or down as the case might be.

With its last major refit back in the mid-forties, it was perhaps a little dated in its style of decor if not in its upkeep, but it was a gracious style complemented by a standard of service which also belonged to a past era. Sinclair employees were there to serve, and would do so with courtesy, efficiency and at least an outward show of interest, old Henry Sinclair had ordained—a maxim passed down via his son to his grandson, and followed to the letter. Only in Ross Sinclair had the unswerving adherence to an old order been in any way questioned. The days were gone, he had stated firmly at twenty-five, when the pace of life allowed for such extremes of customer indulgence. In this modern age profits lay in the fast turnover, the consolidation of closely related departments and better utilisation of floor space. He had outlined a plan for restructuring the whole store, both in design and in management—kicking it into the twentieth century, he had called it. Kerry could still recall the harsh words which had passed between father and son before Ross had finally thrown in the towel and taken himself off to the States to make his own way. Remember, too, the way she had hated the latter for his total disregard of family loyalty. Not that she had ever really cared for him very deeply—any more than he had for her. Circumstances had not favoured a close relationship.

Kerry had been fourteen years old when her mother had met and married Andrew Sinclair. Scarcely able to remember her own father, Kerry had in no way resented the acquisition of a new one. Twenty years older than her mother, Andrew had seemed the kindliest, most indulgent of men—an opinion she had found no cause to change over the last ten years. Ross had been the only fly in the ointment. At twenty-two he had been as far removed from the nice older brother image as it was possible to get. Arrogant, self-opinionated and too clever by half, had been her summing up on their first meeting. While not obviously and openly opposed to the marriage, he had yet managed to transmit the impression that he suspected his stepmother of ulterior motives in marrying a man so many years her senior.

Whether at thirty-one he would have mellowed at all was open to doubt. Men like Ross Sinclair grew harder with time, not softer—the very fact that he had not even bothered to contact her before the funeral served to underline that fact. In four days not even a cable acknowledging hers. Until a few moments ago she had not even been certain he would bother to put in an appearance at all. He certainly had not bothered four years ago when her mother had been killed in a riding accident. Just a formal letter of condolence and nothing since. But there had been nothing in it for him, had there? This time was different.

People were pressing in to speak to her, touching her hand in the tentative manner of those not knowing quite what to say in the presence of bereavement. Andrew's two cousins waited by the cars. Minor shareholders in Sinclairs, they were his only surviving relatives apart from Ross, and very much alike in their dark suits and trilby hats. Also in their sixties, they were both bachelors, and looked it. The brothers Grimm, Ross had once called them in Kerry's hearing, and she had to admit that it suited them. Neither was exactly renowned for humour.

A small party of mourners was coming back to the house for the mandatory funeral feast—although in this particular case they might be disappointed as she had told Mrs Payne not to go to a lot of trouble. The house itself now belonged to Ross, she assumed. At least, there was no reason to believe otherwise. Had Andrew ever had any intention of attempting to cut off his son in favour of others he would surely have given some hint over the years. So far as she knew, he had not made a new will after Ross left, and in the old one, although her mother had been well provided for, the main bulk of the estate went to Ross.

Anyway, all would become clear tomorrow when Mr Watling, Andrew's solicitor, read it out to those concerned. Not at all a common occurrence, Kerry understood from what he had said yesterday, but for some reason he seemed to think it would be better done that way on this occasion. Perhaps some legal jargon which needed explanation for the layman—or woman—to understand properly.

Another hand touched her arm, this time with a firmness of purpose which brought her head round towards the newcomer sharply. Ross was unsmiling but otherwise singularly lacking in any obvious evidence of mourning, his suit a pale grey stripe which sat well across the broad shoulders. Even though she was wearing fairly high heels he was still some few inches taller, his mouth just about on a level with her eyes. She lifted them to meet his own steady grey ones, aware of a faint quiver somewhere deep down as she did so.

'If you're travelling back to the house I may as well come with you,' he said. 'I came by cab from the station.'

There were a dozen things Kerry wanted to say right at that moment, but conscious of the people about them she bit them back, indicating the first of the two limousines with a slight wave of her free hand.

'We'll take that one. The others can follow on.'

The cousins watched them coming with identical expressions, obviously uncertain as to how to greet the return of this prodigal son. Ross removed the dilemma for them with a simple 'How are you?', opening the rear door of the car for Kerry to precede him inside as they found predictable answers. 'Good, so we'll see you back at the house,' he said before following her.

Kerry leaned back against the soft leather as the car drew away, unable to bring herself to turn her head and look at him directly.

'You only just made it. How did you know what time the funeral was?'

'I phoned Watling from Heathrow early this morning right after I landed,' he said. 'It was touch and go whether I'd make the train in time.'

Kerry said low-toned, 'I don't suppose it occurred to you to phone the house and let me know you were at least in the country?'

'It occurred to me.' His own tone was dry. 'As I said, it was early, and I wasn't all that sure of my welcome. Six years is a long time.'

'Isn't it.' She made no attempt to keep the irony from her voice. 'It's a relief to know you got my cable.'

'Yesterday afternoon. Last night by your reckoning. I've been out of town for some days.'

'Oh?' This time she did look at him, seeing the tautness of his features in a sudden new light. 'I didn't realise.'

'No way you could have done.'

'No.' There seemed little else to say on the subject at the moment. Where he had been had no bearing on the matter. He had got here in time and that was something to be thankful for. 'You must be tired after flying all night,' she added. 'Especially coming on top of the shock like that.'

'Yes, it was a shock.' The smile came faintly, without humour. 'I always took it he'd go on till he was eighty at least. The Sinclairs are a long-lived line.'

'It was a heart attack,' Kerry proffered. 'A massive one, apparently. Doctor Simmons said he could have done nothing for him even if he'd been with him at the time.'

'I imagine not. Where did it happen?'

'In bed.' She tried to keep her voice unemotional. 'He complained of indigestion after dinner and went to bed early. I found him next morning. I thought he'd overslept until . . .'

'It can't have been very pleasant for you,' he said quietly as her voice trailed away. 'Even worse if he'd been your own father, of course, but . . .'

'The fact that he wasn't really made very little difference,' Kerry interrupted on a curt note. 'Personally, I never noticed blood being so much thicker than water!' She broke off abruptly, biting her lip. 'I'm sorry, that was a tasteless remark.'

He shrugged. 'If I'd been implying what you appear to think I was I'd have deserved it. Let's forget it, shall we.' It was a statement, not a question. 'Do you still have Mrs Payne?'

'Yes—although she doesn't come in quite as much these days. Since Mom died we haven't done a lot of entertaining.'

Ross made no comment on that; she hadn't really expected one. Silence settled between them for the moment. Kerry studied the passing view from the window at her side, looking out across the town to the hills rising in the distance. Industrial though Medfield might be, it had one of the finest settings in the whole of the Yorkshire county. Hailing from a softer landscape further south herself, she had fallen in love with the rugged moors and green valleys surrounding her new home from the first. Whatever happened she would not be leaving this place. After nine years she belonged.

'I'd hardly have known you if it hadn't been for the hair,' said the man at her side unexpectedly, bringing her attention back inside the car again. 'That coppery colour always was pretty unusual. The style's different, though.'

She was surprised he had remembered that much. 'I had it cut a couple of years ago,' she said, pushing the curved ends back from her jawline. 'It was too long and too thick to put up properly, and you know how your father liked a neat appearance around the Store.'

The grey eyes narrowed a fraction. 'You worked at the Store?'

'Yes.' Kerry hesitated before adding on a faintly defensive note, 'I was his P.A.'

This time there was no visible reaction. 'He must have had a lot of faith in you.'

'We worked well together, if that's what you mean.'

'Shared opinions?'

'To a great extent.'

'I see.' It was his turn to pause. 'And now?'

'That rather depends on circumstances,' she came back cautiously, and saw his mouth take on a sardonic slant.

'You mean if I inherit you might have to rethink your future.'

She sidestepped the question. 'I don't think there's much doubt about the question of inheritance. You're the last of the Sinclair line. No matter how your father felt, he would never have contemplated putting the continuance of the name at risk.'

'You think you knew him so well?'

'Perhaps better than you did.' It was out before she had time to think about it, sharp and cutting and hinting of something she preferred not to probe too deeply. She felt herself flush and quickly carried on. 'Living alone with someone in the same house for four years has to bring a degree of closeness.'

'I lived alone in the same house with him for twelve years,' he returned dryly, 'and I can't say that enhanced our relationship any.'

'Because you were too much alike,' she said. 'You both wanted your own way all the time.'

His laugh was short. 'I seem to remember you once called me a bigheaded bully. I'll bet you never applied a term like *that* to Dad.'

'If I called you that it was probably because you were,' Kerry retorted, refusing to allow him to disconcert her. 'Either that or you ignored me altogether.'

'Not possible. Who could ignore a snooty-nosed little madam who looked at you as though you'd just crawled out from under a slab!' Humour had crept into the line of his mouth, relaxing his features in a way which cancelled out her own smart retort. 'Maybe I asked for it; I don't know. Handling a teenage stepsister was totally beyond me.'

Kerry studied him for a long moment, suspecting ridicule yet not finding any trace of it. 'I wasn't snooty,' she said at last. 'I was shy. You were grown-up and you belonged. It was all new to me. I'd never lived in a house the size of Underwood before, nor gone to quite such a select school. I was overawed by everything those first months, but I couldn't bear anyone to know that, so I put on an act. I never realised it was such a good one.'

'Believe me, it was.' His smile was genuine, warming her out of the depression of the last few days. 'And in my case it never seemed to relax. Pity it had to take an occasion like this to break the ice.'

'Yes.' Impulsively she added, 'You should have come back before, Ross. He would have welcomed you with open arms.'

'Only provided I was willing to accept his way of looking at things. I couldn't pretend to do that, so I stayed away. We corresponded.'

'Did you?' Kerry was taken aback. 'I never realised that.'

'Oh, it didn't happen very often. Not from either side. I guess you're right, we were too much alike basically to make any real overtures. Perhaps if I'd made the first move towards a reconciliation we might have found an effective compromise.'

'But you'd made your own life over there and didn't want to take the chance of losing what you'd gained only to find yourself back to square one?' she hazarded, and received a wry inclination of the dark head.

'Something like that. I got where I wanted to go, learned what I needed to learn.'

'And now?'

His shoulders lifted. 'Like you said, it depends on circumstances. From what Watling said this morning on the phone, I'm certainly mentioned in Dad's will, but that's as much as I know. He could just have left me his best wishes—or his worst ones.'

'Would you be prepared to contest if he'd left you out?'

'No.' The negative was firm. 'I'm not exactly destitute, and my job is still open.'

'What exactly is your job?' Kerry asked with some interest.

'I'm General Manager of the Detroit branch of a large

group.' It was said without particular inflection.

'That's pretty far up the ladder for thirty-one,' she commented, thinking of Sinclairs' management, not one of whom was below fifty.

'Promotion comes fast over there.'

'Not unless it's merited, surely?'

'Okay, so I hit the right circuits. The next logical move is a transfer to Head Office in New York, and I can't say that holds much appeal. I'd rather be where the action is.'

'A very slick and efficient action, I imagine.'

'Very. Makes the set-up at Sinclairs look positively antiquated.' He glanced at her. 'Unless there've been any changes for the better.'

'Some.' She was cautious. 'Probably not along your lines.'

'Tell me one.'

'Well, we installed new escalators last year throughout.'

'And not before time. What else?'

'Redecoration. Modernisation of the restaurant kitchen.'

'I was talking about organisation—operational improvements.'

'I know you were.' Kerry tried hard to keep any note of apology from her tone. 'Profits are still good enough to belie any need for radical change.'

'Only because Dad never took anything much out of the business himself. He never needed to. He didn't run the Store as a business, he ran it as a hobby.'

'The other directors don't complain.'

'Why should they? They make a very comfortable living for very little return. God help everyone if they finish up with the controlling interest!'

Kerry shook her head. 'I'm sure that won't happen.'

'We'll wait and see.'

The car slowed to make the turn out of the broad leafy roadway into the long curving drive leading up to the house.

Ross leaned forward a little to catch a first glimpse of the weathered grey stone, expression undergoing a faint change as the graceful lines came into view. To Kerry nine years ago, the house had looked big enough and grand enough for a palace. It still looked large and imposing, but she was accustomed to the sight and no longer intimidated by it. She had learned to think of Underwood as home, and to love it as such. Yet would she still have that right at this time tomorrow? Andrew would not have left her unprovided for, she knew, but money wasn't everything. Her whole life was about to undergo its second radical change and she dreaded it.

'What happened to your luggage?' she asked as the car drew to a halt before the jutting stone porch with a satisfying crunching of gravel beneath the tyres.

'I had it sent straight on here from the station.' Ross got out first and turned back to help her out, closing the door and giving the driver a nod of dismissal. Standing there so close at her side he appeared taller than ever, his body lean yet with a suggestion of muscularity beneath the beautifully cut suit. She caught a faint whiff of aftershave, subtle and expensive. Looking at him, one would never have guessed that he had travelled solidly throughout the night. He must have shaved on the train to present such a clean-cut appearance, and that in itself was no mean feat considering the size and sheer inconvenience of the average British Rail toilet.

The second car arrived as theirs made the sweeping turn around the central flower bed to leave, coming to a stop to disgorge its half dozen passengers with varying degrees of agility and alacrity. The cousins were first out, standing silently by while first the Vicar and then three ageing friends of the family followed suit. The former never had a lot to say for themselves, even at board meetings. Without Andrew they appeared totally lost, uncertain as to what even the next move should be.

Ross once again solved the problem for them by making a move indoors, his hand lightly under Kerry's elbow. The big oak-panelled hall looked warm and inviting with its huge vase of amber chrysanthemums glowing on the curved table at the foot of the angled staircase. Without hesitation he crossed and opened the double doors on the right, stepping into the lovely, high-ceilinged drawing room as if it were only yesterday since he had last done so.

'Sherry?' he asked. 'I'm having a whisky. I need it.'

The next half hour followed a predictable and established pattern. Kerry kept herself occupied handing round the plates of sandwiches and vol-au-vents, etcetera, prepared by Mrs Payne, serving coffee to those who wanted it, and more sherry to those who did not. The Vicar joined Ross at the whisky decanter with little urging, excusing the indulgence with a reference to the coolness of the wind on this fine autumn morning.

'A great pity,' he kept saying, shaking his head in sad contemplation of the loss they had all sustained. 'A good man, your father, a very good man. The parish won't be the same without him!'

Ross had a quiet word with the cousins in a corner, finally despatching them and the others with an ease which bespoke long practice in dispersing awkward gatherings. The former would no doubt be back tomorrow for the reading of the will, but until then the house was free of visitors.

Apart from Ross himself, Kerry found herself thinking. Yet he could hardly be called a visitor in what was surely now his own property. Until this moment she had not considered the question of where he would be spending the night—or any subsequent ones, if it came to that. Not that it made any difference. Mrs Payne could make up the bed in his old room overlooking the rose garden.

'You will be staying here, of course,' she asked just to make certain, and saw his brows lift a fraction.

'You'd rather I went to a hotel?'

'Why on earth should you do that?'

'Appearances, maybe.'

She looked at him blankly for a moment before realising what he was getting at. 'Don't be ridiculous,' she said. 'So far as anyone is concerned, we're practically brother and sister.'

His lips twisted. 'You're twenty-three, not fourteen, and a very attractive young woman. This town always had a puritanical streak.'

'Not to the extent of believing what you're implying might be believed if we both ocupy the same house overnight.'

'One night, maybe. What price the same forbearance if you turn out to be right about Dad's intentions?'

Her head lifted a little. 'I shan't be here then, shall I? The estate will be yours.'

'And you think I'd expect you to leave?'

Kerry lifted her shoulders rather helplessly. 'I hadn't really thought beyond the funeral yet. There's been so much to do these last few days.'

'Things I should have been doing if I'd been here.' He lit a cigarette from the box on the sofa table, holding it in thoughtful contemplation between two uplifted fingers as he exhaled the smoke. 'So far as I'm concerned, this is your home for as long as you want to make it. Dad will have provided for you, come what may. He was very fond of you.'

'I know.' She said it softly. 'Can we leave it until tomorrow when we'll know just what is going to happen?'

'Sure.' He paused, studying her, expression enigmatic. 'Which leaves us with the rest of today. Personally, I could use some sleep. I didn't get much on the flight. How about dinner tonight?'

'I didn't ask Mrs Payne to stay, but I can cook a meal for the two of us.'

'I meant to go out for it. It's midweek; we don't have to reserve a table anywhere. We can make the choice later.' Ross registered her reaction with a questioning look. 'You don't fancy that?'

'Not on the day of your father's funeral,' she admitted. 'We're supposed to be in mourning, not gadding about the town.'

'I said a meal, not a jamboree.' He sounded suddenly intolerant. 'It's possible to mourn someone without becoming a recluse for weeks after it.'

'There's a difference between your kind of mourning and mine, obviously,' she came back stiffly.

'Obviously.' He gave a resigned sigh. 'All right, so we stay in. I hope you're a good cook these days. I don't seem to remember your occasional culinary efforts as examples of great art.'

Kerry had to smile. 'I agree, they weren't. I think you'll find I've improved. Your father actually preferred my cooking to Mrs Payne's.'

'He was biased.' There was an odd quality to his answering smile. 'I'll reserve opinion. Do I use my old room?'

Kerry stirred herself. 'Just give me a moment to see Mrs Payne first. Not having heard from you it seemed pointless preparing one in advance, but it won't take long.'

The housekeeper was in the large sunny kitchen, humming a tune to herself as she loaded the dishwasher. Having a family of her own to look after, she had never lived in, but commuted several days a week from the other side of town. She was an unfailingly cheerful woman in her sixties.

'Bed's already made up,' the other said in answer to her query. 'Did it when Mr Ross's cases came up from t' station.' Her glance held curiosity. 'Suppose he'll be staying for good now?'

'I'm not quite sure what his plans are,' Kerry replied carefully. 'You don't need to stay on today, Mrs Payne. I shan't be going in to the Store, so I can take care of dinner.'

'Wouldn't mind an afternoon off,' the other agreed. 'What about lunch?'

'I doubt if either of us will want anything else to eat for hours.' On impulse Kerry added, 'Take tomorrow off too if you like. There won't be much for you to do.'

Ross was standing at the window looking out on to the long sweep of lawn down to the belt of trees which formed the outer limits of the formal garden on this side of the house. Beyond them lay the tennis courts, and beyond that more trees flanking the side road. Altogether Underwood boasted more than three and a half acres of grounds, much of it grassed. It took the hired gardener an age to get round the whole lot, even with the aid of the huge motor mower. Andrew had often threatened to sell some of it off, but he hadn't meant it. The house and land had been in the family far too long to start cutting it up without absolute necessity.

'Your room is ready,' Kerry said. 'It's as you left it. Mrs Payne put the clothes you didn't take with you in wardrobe bags against the dust, but they've been aired pretty often.'

'Did I leave so much?' Ross asked, turning back into the room. 'I don't remember.'

'A couple of suits, odd shirts and slacks—I'm not really sure.'

'No matter. I'll be able to see for myself.' He ran a hand through his hair in a gesture which bespoke weariness. 'If I haven't surfaced by five or so give me a call, will you? Sorry to be a drag, but I'm shattered.'

Shattered, shocked and not all that sure of the future, Kerry summed up judiciously to herself. Left alone, she stood irresolutely for a moment wondering what to do with herself for the next few hours, half wishing she had not elected to take the whole day off. It was too late now. She was stuck with the decision. There were some household accounts still to go through; she could while away an hour or so with those, she supposed. A clear presentation of outstanding debts would be required anyway by Mr Watling as executor, tomorrow morning. Andrew had taken care to leave his family free of the burden of administration. Even the will had been lodged with his solicitor rather than in the study safe. Not that he had made any secret of it. She had known for years that Mr Watling would be taking care of things when it became necessary. What she, nor anyone else for that matter, had not anticipated was that the necessity might arise so soon.

The large, gilt-edged mirror flanking the doorway reflected her approach, a slim, trim figure in the smoothly fitting black dress, face framed by inward-turning copper hair. Green eyes looked steadily back at her, revealing little of what was going on inside her head.

A very attractive young woman, Ross had called her. Being no more prone to false modesty than she was to undue conceit, Kerry was not unaware that others considered her so too, yet she had never felt quite the same quick glow at that knowledge. Ross was different. Six years had added far more than mere age. There was an assurance about him that was far removed from the brash confidence of former days. She wondered about the women in his life. No doubt there had been some. He was not only a vitally attractive man but also a successful one—the kind of combination to which most female hearts warmed. Had it been a woman who had kept him out of touch with the world these last few days? Probably she would never know. She wasn't even sure she wanted to know. Ross Sinclair was back in her life, and a gap she had never fully acknowledged was finally filled again. For how long was anyone's guess.

It was six-thirty before he came downstairs again. He looked refreshed, and very much more at home in a pair of brown slacks and a silky white sweater, the thick dark hair smoothly brushed.

'You should have woken me,' he said, coming through to the kitchen where Kerry was preparing their meal, and leaning against the doorjamb to watch her. 'I didn't intend sleeping this long.'

'You obviously needed it,' she pointed out on a practical note. 'Better to waken naturally than to be jerked out of it before you were ready. I've never flown enough to experience jet lag myself, but I've heard enough about it.'

'Disorientation,' he said. 'So far as my brain is concerned it's still around about lunchtime.'

Kerry smiled. 'I don't suppose your stomach will register the distinction providing it gets fed. I can have this ready in half an hour. I only have the rice to do.'

Ross sniffed the air appreciatively. 'Smells good! What is it?'

'Only chicken à la king, I'm afraid. I thought there was a chance you might just sleep the clock round.'

'And leave you with a burned offering. The chicken will be fine. How about a bottle of wine to go with it?'

'Lovely. The cellar key's in its usual place.'

'Where else?' His tone was dry.

They ate at seven in the soft evening light of the dining room. Without thinking about it, Kerry had set Ross a place at the head of the polished mahogany table, placing herself on his left. She saw him eye the gleaming silver and sparkling glassware with a faint twist to his lips as he took up the heavy damask napkin and shook it open across his knees, his glance lifting briefly to the multi-faceted chandelier hanging overhead.

'I'd almost forgotten what gracious living was like,' he admitted. 'My apartment in Detroit has every conceivable mod-con, but it's almost the mirror image of every other place in the block.'

'I suppose you'll have to go back if only to finalise things,' Kerry said. 'Is that likely to take long?'

'We were going to leave that subject alone until tomorrow,' he reminded her without altering his expression. 'I can't make any plans without knowing just what Dad's will says.'

'No, of course not. I'm sorry.' Kerry was certain he had nothing to doubt but refrained from repeating the assurance. 'Tell me about the store in Detroit. How big is it?'

'Three times the square footage of Sinclairs. A block wide by four floors high—no, five by British standards. We count the ground as first over there.'

'That's a lot of responsibility.'

'I have an excellent executive staff to work with.'

She longed to ask him if he would regret giving it all up, but considering what he had said a few moments ago the question was better kept to herself for the present. Perhaps he even privately hoped that his father had removed the responsibility for Sinclairs' future from his shoulders. His life in the States sounded full and satisfying, and he had the gratification of knowing he had achieved everything by his own efforts. That must mean a lot to a man like Ross.

Kerry had her opinion reinforced during the meal as he continued to respond to her questioning. By the time they finished dessert she had a basic grasp of the differences between American and British retail management and thought them minor enough on the surface to allow for interchange without undue reorganisation. They took their coffee through to the drawing room, where Ross put a match to the ready-laid fire, sitting back into the depths of the brocade sofa with a small sound of satisfaction as the flames sprang alive.

'A British autumn has a lot to be said for it,' he remarked.

'I prefer spring myself,' Kerry returned lightly. 'That's a beginning, this is an end.' The arm he had thrown casually along the sofa back was almost behind her shoulders. If she leaned back as he was doing himself she would feel it against the nape of her neck. She stayed as she was, head bent a little in contemplation of her coffee cup. 'According to the long-range forecast it's going to be a hard winter.'

Ross laughed with a hint of malice. 'Now I know I'm back! Tell me about yourself. What have you been doing these last few years? Apart from working with Dad, I mean.'

'Not a lot.' It was true. Sinclairs had filled her world as it had filled Andrew's. If Ross's theory of the Store being a hobby rather than a busines proposition was correct, then it had been an all-consuming one. 'I'm in the Medfield Amateur Dramatic Society.'

'There has to be more to life than amateur dramatics.' The pause was brief. 'What about boy-friends?'

Kerry lifted an eyebrow. 'Is that asked in the spirit of brotherly interest, or just plain curiosity?'

'I'm not your brother.' This time his tone was almost brusque. 'There's no blood tie.'

'I wasn't forgetting,' she came back quietly. 'It was supposed to be a joke.'

'My sense of humour never did stretch quite that far.' He studied her averted face for a moment, then reached forward without warning and took the cup and saucer from her unresisting hand to deposit them on the low inlaid table in front of her. The arm along the sofa back dropped to her shoulders, his hand curving the line of her jaw to turn her head towards him. The grey eyes held an unfathomable expression. 'I couldn't do this to my sister,' he added softly, and kissed her.

As kisses went this one didn't last long, yet it stirred something in her rarely stirred before. For a moment she was still in his grasp, her lips half parting in involuntary response, softening beneath his in a manner far removed from simple family affection. Recollection brought her hands up to his chest to push him away in haste and confusion. She could hardly bring herself to meet his eyes.

'That wasn't funny either,' she got out.

'It wasn't meant to be. I just felt like doing it.' Cynicism touched his mouth. 'You wanted it too.'

'No!' The denial was torn from her. 'I never thought of you that way!'

'Nor I you—before.' He made no attempt to touch her again, watching her face with that same faint smile. 'The only thing I wanted to do to you in the past was knock some of that righteous condemnation out of you. Have you any idea what it was like having a kid your age criticise every idea I ever had?' He shook his head as she opened her mouth on the denial. 'Not in so many words, maybe, but those eyes of yours spoke volumes. You've learned to hide your feelings more these days, only physical attraction has a way of taking you unawares. I know. It happened to me too, the minute I set eyes on you again.'

'Ross.' Her voice was shaky. 'We cremated your father only this morning.'

'And life still goes on. Don't worry, I don't intend besmirching the family honour by making love to you. I just needed to prove something to myself, that's all.'

'Such as what?'

'That's my affair.'

'I think it has to be mine too.'

'Because I kissed you? Don't read too much into too little. It won't happen again.'

'I wish it hadn't happened at all,' she said unhappily. 'I don't understand you.'

'You're not on your own.' Ross took up the coffee pot to refill both cups, handing her hers with an edge of brusqueness. 'Drink that and stop dithering. With any luck I'll be on my way before the end of the week.'

'Whose luck?' she demanded, only just beginning to suspect what might really be bothering him. 'Yours or mine?'

His glance came back to her, semi-mocking. 'It's not beyond the realms of possibility. Tonight I sat at the head of the table and still felt like a visitor being indulged by the mistress of the house. Dad could have felt the same way.'

'Like a visitor?'

'That you fitted the position. Stop fencing. We both know what we're talking about.'

'I don't know what's in the will,' she denied with forced calm. 'Not in any sense. Perhaps if I'd agreed four years ago when your father asked me to change my name to his by deed poll there might have been something for you to be afraid of, but no way would he leave the estate outside the Sinclair name. I keep telling you that.' She paused, feeling the bitterness of disillusionment creeping through her. 'I was wrong about you; I thought you'd changed. But you haven't. Not basically. You never had any feeling for your father, only for what you considered your rights. I wish I could believe he would have disinherited you!'

'I'm sure you do.' Any cosy camaraderie there might have been between them had long since flown. The grey eyes were steely. 'Maybe that's why we're attracted to each other—like calling to like. Naturally Dad wouldn't have seen you that way. You've had four years to make yourself indispensable to him, and you obviously took full advantage.'

The only thing worse than being in the wrong, Kerry acknowledged in pain, was to have someone imagine you were with no way of convincing them otherwise. Tomorrow might remove some of the doubt, but nothing was going to convince him he was totally incorrect about her motives in taking the interest she had in the business. Yet there had been a moment in the car coming back here this morning when she had been convinced they were on the same wavelength at last. False hopes. Too much time had passed for that to ever happen now.

'I'm going to my room,' she said huskily. 'Mr Watling will be here at ten. I thought we'd use the study.'

'I'm sure you thought of everything.' He didn't get up. 'Have a restful night!'

Upstairs in her own delightful bedroom, Kerry sat on the silk-draped bed and contemplated the immediate future with grim purpose. After this there was no way she could stay here at Underwood, nor work for Sinclairs. She would need a job of some kind regardless. That might not prove too difficult; she could certainly offer experience of the retail trade. Outside Medfield, though. The town wasn't large enough to offer total insulation from her past life. London perhaps—that was anonymous enough. A completely fresh start. The thought held few attractions.

CHAPTER TWO

THERE was no sign of Ross when she got down at eight, but indications in the kitchen that someone had made coffee and scrambled eggs. Kerry did the same for herself, wondering where he had got to. With his inner clock still out no doubt he had found sleep hard to come by. But certainly no more than she had. It had been almost dawn before she had managed to doze at all.

He came in at a little after nine, casual suede jacket swinging loose from his broad-shouldered frame.

'I took a walk,' he said. 'It's been a long time since I did that just for the pleasure of it. There's a real nip in the air this morning.' He looked at her sitting silently there at the breakfast room table and his mouth took on a wry slant. 'I was a brute last night. Can we forget it?'

The apology, such as it was, disconcerted her. Whatever she had been expecting from him, a retraction was certainly not on the list. Yet had he actually retracted anything when it came down to it? Forget it, he had said, not I was wrong.

'I usually walk Sunday mornings,' she said, sidestepping the question. 'There's something satisfying about getting up early when you don't actually have to.'

'You think so too?' He took his cue from her, apparently unperturbed by her failure to respond. 'Is there any coffee left?'

'There is some, it might not be very hot.' At any other time Kerry would have offered to make some fresh, this time she kept her seat. 'You'll need a cup.'

Dark brows lifted a fraction, but he made no comment,

moving forward to put a hand to the pot. 'You're right, it's not very hot. Why don't you use the percolator?'

'Because I prefer an earthenware pot.'

'You can buy earthenware percolators.'

'Ceramic,' she corrected patiently. 'And we happen to already have two in stainless steel.' She registered the possessive pronoun with a sense of constraint, aware that he had noted it too. So what did he expect? She was accustomed to saying we in relation to Andrew and herself. One didn't break a habit overnight.

'I'm going up to change,' he said. 'I'll see you in the study at ten.'

Less than three quarters of an hour, Kerry reflected, watching him go with a dry little ache at the back of her throat, and then they would know. If Mr Watling hadn't decided to make a production of it, they would know already. There had to be a good reason, of course, and that suggested something not quite as straightforward as one might hope. But not disinheritance. That was unthinkable. Andrew wouldn't have, *couldn't* have done such a thing.

The solicitor arrived at five minutes to the hour, looking, Kerry thought, somewhat less than happy to be here. An old family associate, he had known Ross since he was born, but his greeting this morning held an element of repression.

The study was Kerry's favourite room. Book-lined, leather-chaired and thickly carpeted, it welcomed both the browser and the worker. The nineteenth-century desk under the bow window still held the pipe and tobacco pouch her stepfather had used the night he died. She saw Ross look at them and compress his lips, whether in annoyance because they had not been cleared away or disturbance over the memories they provoked she had no way of knowing.

'Shouldn't we wait for the others?' she found herself

blurting out without meaning to as the solicitor opened his briefcase to take out the folded parchment sheets he had come to read to them, and received an oddly resigned look from the latter.

'There are no others, my dear. Apart from a few minor bequests which can be dealt with quite simply, you and Ross are the only legatees.'

Afterwards, thinking back to this moment and remembering Ross's sudden movement, she knew then that he had already guessed what was to come; but right now all she could feel was relief that her faith in her stepfather had been vindicated. He had not rejected his only son.

Sitting at the desk in Andrew Sinclair's chair, the solicitor cleared his throat before beginning to read from the papers he held in his hand. The first part was predictable: five hundred pounds to Mrs Payne in recognition of her services to the family over the years; the same to the gardener; a rather more substantial sum to a charity he had favoured spasmodically during his life, and a donation to the local Conservative club.

A pause at that point indicated that the next part of the will was of more import. Mr Watling cleared his throat again before continuing: The residue of the estate, I give and bequeath to be shared equally between my son Ross Sinclair and my stepdaughter Kerry Rendal on the understanding that each shall reside at Underwood for no less than nine months of every year, and each take an active seat on the board of Sinclairs Department Store. Signed and witnessed this seventh day of August nineteen-seventy-four.'

August '74, thought Kerry dazedly when she could think at all. Barely three months after her mother's accident. But why? How could Andrew have done such a thing? To put a curb on Ross, perhaps? To stop him taking control of Sinclairs and turning it into something he himself would have hated? Such faith in her loyalty moved her immeasurably even while her mind rejected the whole idea. Half the house would have been bad enough, but *every*thing! Oh no, Andrew. No!

'Congratulations.' Ross's tone was flat. 'I guess we just became partners.'

She knew then that he was going to fight—not the will, because that was probably unassailable, but she herself. The knowledge tautened her throat. She made herself meet his eyes, anticipating the expression she could see in them. But whatever his initial reactions, he had himself under control now, face revealing nothing. Kerry held up her hands in unconscious appeal.

'I don't know what to say.'

'Try thank you,' he suggested. 'If there is an after-life he might just hear you.'

Mr Watling coughed uncomfortably, sensing the enmity with obviously no idea what to do about it. 'If you'd both like to come down to the office at your convenience we can go into actual facts and figures.' There was a brief pause before he continued, 'One thing I ought to make clear right away. It's going to be necessary to sell some stock outside of Sinclairs in order to meet taxes on the estate. That won't exactly leave you paupers, but an overall increase in profit from Sinclair stock wouldn't come amiss.'

So that was it. Kerry drew in a silent breath. Andrew had known this would come. He was too shrewd a man not to have realised that CTT would eat up some capital and therefore necessitate adjustment from other quarters. What he had determined was that any change in policy should not be of so radical a nature as to alter the whole image of Sinclairs, and for that he had relied on her intervention. Well, she would not let him down. He had trusted her and she would now repay that trust to the very best of her ability, regardless of how Ross felt about it.

Despite her determination, it was with some trepidation that she saw the solicitor off the premises, all too conscious of the waiting presence at her back. Ross was still standing in the study doorway when she turned. He indicated the room behind him with a gesture of one hand.

'We have things to talk about.'

Kerry passed him with an outward air of composure, swinging as she reached the desk to lean her weight back agaist both hands and return his gaze unflinchingly.

'Well?'

'I'm prepared to pay you above market value for thirty per cent of your forty in Sinclair stock,' he said without preamble. 'You'd still hold a seat on the board, of course, along with the cousins.'

As a minority shareholder with little power. Kerry let nothing of her reaction show in her face. 'Can you afford to buy me out?'

His face darkened. 'Where and how I get the money is my business. I want that stock.'

'I know you do.' Her voice was quiet. 'Trust you to find a way round mere wording. The answer is no.'

'Why?'

'Because your father obviously didn't want you to have that much power. Given a free hand you'd restructure the whole organisation. I agree there's room for improvement, but not at the cost of everything he worked to maintain. We attract a great deal of our custom because we offer the kind of service the chains can't. Take that away and we have to compete on the same level.'

'It didn't take long, did it?' he said softly, and then as her brows drew together, 'To acquire the royal We.'

Kerry flushed. 'Your father always encouraged me to think of Sinclairs from that angle. He believed it showed involvement.' She paused, searching the angular features with a look of appeal. 'Ross, can't we talk out this whole affair without bitterness creeping in? I can guess how you feel, but . . .'

'Can you? I doubt it.' He shook his head impatiently. 'Feelings don't enter into it. There's more potential in that store than Dad, you, the Barratts or anyone else ever dreamed of, and I'm going to realise it if it's the last thing I do!'

'Not too far, you're not. And don't rely on the cousins either. They have a liking for the old order too.'

'So I'll fight all three of you if necessary.'

'You can try.'

He gave her a long appraising look, then suddenly shrugged. 'I guess we're going to have to take it day by day. Starting today, I want to take a look round the Store and get an overall picture.'

He was right, Kerry acknowledged, there was no point in continuing the discussion—if it could fairly be called that. Later, when they had both cooled down, would be a better time. In some ways it might even have been better if Ross had inherited no part in the Store because then he could have snapped his fingers at the lot of them and gone back to his own life. Except that she doubted if it would have happened quite that way, despite what he had said in the car yesterday. Not when it came to the point. Sinclairs was a challenge; it always had been a challenge. Only instead of his father he was now up against her. She only hoped she was going to prove equal to the task Andrew had set her.

'What about lunch?' she asked.

'We'll eat there.'

She stirred herself to reach for the telephone. 'I'd better let the manager's dining room staff know we're coming in.'

'I meant in the restaurant. The best way of assessing a department's worth is at first hand.'

'All right.' It was unusual, but Kerry was willing to go

along. 'I'll make sure we have a table reserved. One o'clock?'

'I don't want a table reserving.' He sounded hard and intolerant. 'I don't want any warning given at all. If there's a queue we'll stand in it, I hope anonymously, until a table becomes available. What's good enough for the customer should be good enough for us—and that includes the standard of cooking as well as service.' He paused, eyeing her thoughtfully. 'In fact, it might be better if you took lunch in the manager's dining room and left me to do the sampling alone. No one is likely to recognise me.'

'I don't know about the States, of course, never having been there,' Kerry came back stiffly, 'but that's not the way we do things over here.'

The strong mouth curled. 'You're living in a dream world if you really believe that claptrap. Please yourself. Even if we are spotted there isn't going to be time to do much about it.' He ran a glance over her grey wool suit, lingering for a brief but deliberate moment on her slender, shapely legs neatly shod in matching suede court shoes. 'If you're ready we may as well get straight off.'

Her readiness was material rather than emotional, but not for anything was she going to allow him to guess the state of her mind at this moment. 'I'll get my things,' she said.

Occupying a prominent and central position on High Street, Sinclairs still retained the original Georgian façade, the stonework revealed in all its glory by the recent cleansing it had received. By modern standards, the ground floor windows were limted in their viewing capacity, but in Kerry's estimation more than made up for this lack by the standard and inspired creativeness of the displays within each frame.

Passing along the frontage on their way round to the staff car part at the rear of the store, she saw that the right-hand window immediately flanking the imposing triple main doors appeared to be attracting a lot of attention from passers-by. 'Autumn Leisure', she recalled from the list of projected tableaux sent up recently by the chief dresser. Put in last night after closing in order to present a completed picture to the public this fine Wednesday morning. She must come down and have a closer look at it as soon as the opportunity presented itself. Lester Belton's flair for design was one of the Store's greatest assets, and if his artistic ego needed the occasional managerial boost then it was surely the duty of someone in that upper structure to supply it.

News of the new order of directorship could not possibly have leaked yet, but knowing the grapevine established over years in the place, Kerry doubted if it would take very long. There would be those, she knew, who would look askance at the advent of someone as young as herself on to the board—particularly as she was female into the bargain. Many of Sinclairs' senior staff relished the order Andrew had not seen fit to bring up to date, and would be devastated by the realisation that their former idol had after all possessed feet of clay. Well, like Ross himself, they would have to learn to accept it. She was here and she was staying, come what may.

The man at her side made no comment as he swung the wheel of the Jaguar to turn into the narrow side street. He had driven through the town in the same way, evincing little or no curiosity in the changes which had inevitably taken place since he had last seen Medfield, his only apparent concern in reaching the Store as soon as possible. The car was almost new, silver-grey in colour and possessing every luxury. So far as she was concerned, Ross could have it. The smaller, less sumptuous but equally comfortable Vandem Plas Allegro would suit her fine. She supposed it was permissible to divide actual material assets that way. Short of selling both cars and taking equal shares of the cash involved she could see no other way of settling the issue.

With regard to the rest of their joint inheritance she foresaw few real difficulties. They were required to share the house as a residence, that was all. All? She almost laughed out loud at that point. Underwood was a big place, true, but she doubted if any house could be large enough to hold the two of them in isolation. Unless other arrangements were made, they would share meals and recreation facilities for a start, to say nothing of working space—although it would be easy, she supposed, for one of them to use the study while the other utilised the smaller sitting room should their requirements on that particular score clash. Those were all matters they were going to have to deal with as and when they arose, she decided. Now was hardly the time to be worrying about details of that nature when there was so much else to concern her.

The space allocated to the Chairman was mercifully empty. Ross slid the vehicle into place and switched off the engine, cuff riding up to reveal a solid gold Rolex watch. His suit this morning was a pale silver-blue which toned beautifully with the Jaguar's interior upholstery, modern in cut without being overstated, his shirt a deeper-toned stripe with a plain silk tie. If he really imagined he would not be noticed he had another think coming, Kerry reflected with dry relish. Senior male staff wore dark suits without exception. Only amongst the juniors was a little laxity in that direction smiled upon, and only then so far as a medium grey pinstripe. Women and girls alike all wore the same uniform of tailored grey skirt and white blouse, the latter to be spotless at all times. It was not difficult to imagine the kind of impact the new director would have on the more impressionable younger generation of female staff, even chosen as they were for their lack of latter-day extremities. At thirty-one, Ross was young enough, and certainly attractive enough, to belie the whole image of upper-floor executives.

'The office first, I think,' he said now, glancing at his watch as he got out of the car. 'It's barely twelve. We'll start the tour proper this afternoon.'

'Word will have got round by then,' Kerry pointed out, tongue in cheek. 'Aren't you afraid of a false impression?'

'The kind of assessment I'll be making has nothing to do with staff behaviour,' he retorted hardily. 'They can run about like scalded cats and it won't make a ha'porth of difference, as my grandfather used to say. I'll be looking at displays, utilisation of floor space and general quality of stock rather than checking fingernails.'

'Oh, come on,' Kerry protested mildly. 'Your father never went as far as that!'

'Not so far off it. And stop calling him "my father" every time you want to refer to him. What did you call him when he was alive?'

'Latterly, Andrew,' on a faintly defensive note. 'He preferred it.'

'Then call him that now. I'll know who you're talking about.'

She refrained from further comment, determined not to allow him to get under her skin. Any further, at least, she acknowledged ruefully, than he was already under. The attraction was still there, unweakened by what had passed between them both last night and this morning. It was one other thing she had to fight.

They took the staff lift to the fourth floor, emerging on to the carpeted corridor leading in three directions from this point. Ross took the left-hand turn with the confidence of total memory recall, making no allowance for any possible changeover in office allocation during the last few years. But then why should he? The Chairman's office was right next door to the boardroom, and the latter was not easily relocated.

Arthur Fielding, the Company Secretary, was just emerging from his own office, tall spare figure impeccably clad in dark grey, thinning grey hair brushed carefully across the top of his head. He had been with Sinclairs for more than thirty years all told, and secretary for the last twelve since the retirement of the previous incumbent—an office he would now carry until his own retirement, all being well. His sombre features changed expression as his eyes fell on Ross.

'Welcome home,' he said with some obvious reservation. 'Unfortunate that it had to be in such unhappy circumstances. Your father was a much respected and admired man both in and out of Medfield, Mr Sinclair.'

'Thank you.' Ross shook the respectfully proffered hand, revealing nothing of what he was thinking. 'I'll be needing a detailed statement of our present financial position from you within the next couple of days. Take any help you need in preparing it, but I'd like it on my desk by Friday morning at the latest.'

The possessive pronoun rankled with Kerry, but she refrained from comment. There was nothing to be gained and possibly quite a lot to be lost by airing their differences in public. She waited until they were inside the quiet, cedar-panelled office which had been her stepfather's before saying mildly:

'At the risk of sounding petty, might I point out that this is supposed to be a partnership?'

He swung to look at her then, dropping the sheaf of papers back into the 'In' tray on the big desk, dark brows lifting in a manner which made her squirm.

'Somebody has to take control if we're going to get anything done. You consider yourself better equipped for the job?'

'No, but . . .'

'Either of the cousins, then?'

'No, of course not. In any case they . . .'

'They don't come into it,' he finished for her on the same hard note. 'Too true. This is between the two of us. Well, okay, you're as much at liberty to issue instructions as I am, providing you know what you're doing and why. I'm not attempting to form policy at this point, just trying to get things sorted out to a point where we can all of us see a clear picture. For that I need facts and figures.'

Meeting the scornful grey eyes, Kerry felt shamed. He had so much more experience than she had, to say nothing of the greater moral right.

'I'm sorry,' she offered on impulse. 'You're right, of course.'

'Apology accepted.' He moved round behind the desk and sat down in the swivel chair. 'I take it you have an office of your own?'

Her chin lifted. 'Yes, right next door.'

'That's useful. Is Miss Jardine still here?'

'She retired three years ago. Present secretary is a Mrs Anthony.'

'Age?'

'About fifty-three, I should think. You'd have to ask Personnel. She's very efficient.'

'I'm sure she is.' His tone was dry. 'You must have caused quite a ripple on the upper floor when you came to work here on a regular basis—although I suppose as you were one of the family it was a little different. How long did it take you to persuade Dad to give you a job?'

'I didn't have to ask, he suggested it.' She fought to stay outwardly unmoved. 'Contrary to your obvious opinion, I didn't angle for any share in the Company.'

'You expected nothing?'

'If I'd thought about it at all, which I didn't, not expecting anything like this to happen, I'd have taken it that he would have provided for me, being the kind of man he was, but that's all.'

'So given a choice you wouldn't have wanted this amount of responsibility?'

'No,' she admitted frankly. 'But having been given it I don't intend opting out. I know how Andrew felt about Sinclairs, and I uphold a great many of his ideals.'

'Even though they were for the most part years out of date.' His lips twisted. 'You're going to have to relinquish one or two of them if we're going to get anywhere at all. We're a limited company—the house, etcetera, can't be touched—but we might have to finish up selling the place anyway if we can't lift our joint incomes enough to finance the estate.'

Kerry said thoughtfully, 'I wonder what would happen under those circumstances? The will stipulated we both had to live there nine months of the year in order to inherit at all, which we can hardly do if we had to sell.'

'I don't know. Could call for a court ruling.' Ross moved impatiently. 'It's a hypothetical question right now. Providing you don't block every move I try to make we should be okay. At least we don't have to contend with competition in our own particular field here in Medfield, so nothing we do has to bear immediate comparison. The problem is retaining the department store image while bringing the price margins closer to the chains. We could try joining a buying group on certain lines of stock. Then there's leased shops. Get firms like Susan Small and Mary Quant interested and we stand a good chance of drawing in more chain-orientated customers.'

'That reduces flexibility in our own floor layout.'

'True. But against that you have to consider the advantages of a regular guaranteed rental. So far it's only an idea.'

Among how many others? Kerry wondered. And how far did they go? She supposed she would have to wait to find that out. At least Ross appeared to be trying to find a compromise.

A tap on the communicating door of her own office heralded the tentative entry of Kate Anthony, the latter pausing on the threshold in some small confusion on seeing Ross seated behind the desk.

'I thought I heard voices,' she said. 'I wasn't certain ...'

'We only arrived a few minutes ago,' Kerry said. She performed introductions, watching the older woman's reactions with a certain cynicism. No doubting that Ross had impact on the average female, regardless of age. The normally imperturbable Mrs Anthony looked quite flustered after shaking hands with her new boss.

'I was just about to go to lunch,' she said, 'but if there's anything you need ...'

'Not at present, thanks,' Ross assured her pleasantly. 'Miss Rendal and I are lunching here in the Store shortly, and then we'll be out on the floors most of the afternoon. I'll have some notes for you to type up in the morning, but nothing until then.'

'I've one or two letters which ought to go off today,' Kerry said. 'Perhaps round about four.' She avoided glancing Ross's way. If he hadn't finished his tour by then he would have to continue alone. The normal daily routine still went on despite the winds of change.

Ross remained on his feet as the secretary went out by the way she had come. 'May as well go down now. I had a very early breakfast.'

'And I never offered you any elevenses. Remiss of me.' Her tone was deliberately light. 'It seems to have been that kind of morning.'

'There'll be a lot of others.' His tone was light, but the

words themselves were not meant to be taken lightly. 'Let's go.'

The restaurant was on the second floor just off to the left of the escalator where few people could fail to see the displayed menu. Kerry had not anticipated a queue on a Tuesday lunchtime, and she was not proved wrong. The restaurant itself was approximately half full, the staff coping without difficulty. Recognition brought a look of faint trepidation to the manageress's face, swiftly concealed behind a smile of welcome.

'Nice to have you back, Mr Sinclair,' she said, showing them to a window table. An unobtrusive flick of a finger brought a waitress across to them at once.

Kerry chose the fresh salmon salad as a main course, with fruit juice for starters. After studying the menu for a moment or two longer, Ross opted for steak and kidney pie with a choice of vegetables, starting off with soup of the day which in this case was oxtail. While waiting for the latter to arrive, he extracted a small notebook from an inside pocket and jotted down a couple of observations Kerry could not read upside down.

'You said the place had recently been decorated?' he asked without looking up.

'Yes,' she acknowledged, and then on a sharper note, 'You're not thinking of redoing that, I hope?'

'Not a bit. It suits the era. The lighting on the other side is wrong, though. Green shades give a cold, unwelcoming impression.'

'What would you suggest as an alternative—fluorescents?'

He looked up then, mouth tautened. 'You're spoiling for a fight, aren't you? Save it for tonight, and I'm your man, but let's try and behave rationally while we're on public view.'

It was Kerry who dropped her eyes first. Sarcasm was no

way of getting to him. All that succeeded in doing was to make her feel and look a fool. 'All right,' she said, 'so what colour would you choose?'

'Gold—plus a slightly lowered fitting. On the other hand, would you call this an average occupancy?'

'I suppose so.' The answer was reluctant. 'Saturdays are busiest.'

'Full?'

'Between twelve and one, mostly.'

'One day out of six. Maybe more people prefer the light snack at lunchtime.'

'We don't have any space for a snack bar.'

'Yes, we do. Right here. A partition down the centre, a self-service counter the other side and a different style of seating, and there you have it. Cost minimal. The same kitchen would cater for both outlets.'

Kerry looked for snags and could find no major ones. The restaurant had been running on marginal profits for longer than she could remember, kept alive only for the convenience of those customers who required the service. A snack bar would hold greater appeal for the casual shopper and could even cover possible losses on a reduced capacity restaurant.

'It would mean reorganising the kitchen,' she pointed out, trying not to allow too much enthusiasm to show in her voice. 'But it could work.'

'Approval at last.' He sounded mildly surprised. 'Dad would never have agreed.'

'He didn't have to find extra profits in a hurry.'

'Not that much of a hurry. We need time to consider. I'd like to conduct some market research before any major decisions are taken.'

'How?'

'Customer questionnaire maybe. They're the ones we're catering for, let's find out what they want.'

Kerry looked doubtful. 'You may not find people so willing to spend time filling in questionnaires.'

'So we spread a team around the Store with clipboards, and they do the filling in for them. Make them feel their opinion is important to the Store and there'll be few refusals. We increased turnover by four per cent just by acting on a couple of suggestions which cropped up the most regularly in Detroit. One of them was for a crèche where mothers could leave their offspring while they shopped.'

'We hardly have room for *that* here,' Kerry protested.

'Maybe not, but a perambulator park with attendant might prove a reasonable alternative.'

Not if all the kids started yelling their heads off for absent mothers at the same time, she reflected with irony. Not that a man could be expected to think of that angle.

'I suppose it's worth trying,' she said. 'The whole idea, I mean. Would you do the organising yourself?'

'Hardly. We'd hire expert help.'

'That's going to cost.'

'You have to spend money to make more,' he came back dryly. 'It's a calculated risk.'

He had no criticism to make of the meal when it came, and the standard of service went without question, of course. The moment they had finished coffee he was on his feet ready to go.

'The G.M. first,' he said. 'Still Arnold Gregson, I suppose? Must be getting close to retirement by now.'

'About a year,' Kerry agreed. 'Hoping to take him by surprise?'

The glance he gave her was intolerant. 'Hardly. He'll have known we're in the Store for the past hour or more. We could go back to the office and send for him, I suppose, but seeing we have to pass his door to do it we may as well call on him.'

Ruefully, she said, 'You have a talent for putting people in the wrong.'

'With some it isn't difficult.' He indicated the nearby stairs door. 'Shall we walk up? It's good for the digestion.'

The General Manager was in his office, his greeting to Ross holding the same element of reserve revealed by Arthur Fielding. They both scented change in the air, Kerry thought, and were disturbed by the connotations. She didn't blame them. Ross was enough to disturb anybody with his sweeping 'new broom' manner. So far she was able to go along with the plans he was formulating, but this was only the beginning. Once he really got the bit between his teeth the problems would arise thick and fast, nothing was more certain than that.

CHAPTER THREE

Ross declined the GM's offer to accompany them on their tour of the Store on the grounds that three executives together formed too formal a party. Kerry considered backing out herself and leaving him to it, then decided against it because it would leave her too much in the dark. At least if she were with him she could gain some idea of his reactions to what he saw and be warned of possible trouble areas. Not that she intended blocking any more of his ideas than she absolutely had to in order to keep faith with Andrew. It was the Sinclair image that had been so all-important to her stepfather. Dignity was the keyword, and it was that she must fight to retain against all odds.

Long before the afternoon was over she was beginning to realise just how far those odds were going to be piling up. Ross's comments on layout alone were enough to lift blood pressure sky-high. Staff distribution also came in for criticism. Too many in the wrong place at the wrong time, was only one of the things he had to say. With the staff themselves she considered him far too informal. Juniors particularly needed to look on upper management with a tinging of awe, as creatures from another world—at least that was what Andrew had always said. Right or wrong, it was Store policy for the different levels not to associate too freely.

By four the notebook Ross carried was almost full, and he was by no means through. He agreed, however, to call it a day when Kerry tentatively suggested tea back upstairs, obviously considering he had enough to be going on with.

'You can read the report when it's completed,' he said noncommittally when she asked him for a conclusion on the day's findings. 'It's easier to tie things together on paper.'

He got on the phone to a locally based firm of market researchers when they reached the Chairman's office, arranging for someone to come over the following morning to discuss details. Kate Anthony brought in tea as he finished, the latter beautifully served in Spode china and accompanied by a plate of wafer-thin ham sandwiches plus another of small cakes.

'Standing order with the restaurant,' Kerry explained, seeing the expression on Ross's face as he viewed the repast. 'I didn't get round to cancelling it yet.'

'Then you'd better do it as of now—unless you like a mid-afternoon meal?'

'No,' she denied. 'A drink is all I need.'

'It was all Dad ever needed too. I don't even remember him touching the food. He just liked it to be there in case he felt peckish.'

'We all have our idiosyncrasies,' she returned lightly.

'Some more than others.' He stirred sugar into his cup, regarding her with irony in the line of his mouth. 'Are you going to follow me around all week too?'

She refused to rise to the taunt. 'I doubt it. I have my own work to take care of.'

'Then I can leave the general stuff in your hands and concentrate on completing this,' placing a fleeting hand on the notebook lying on the desk in front of him. 'It's going to take some sorting out.'

'That bad?'

'I told you, wait for the report. Then you'll know all.' He paused. 'What about supper tonight? Want to go out for it?'

Kerry shook her head. 'I've been used to cooking for two.'

'And it's still too close to the funeral.' He gave her no time to reply to that. 'Maybe as well, I'll be working most of the evening. No doubt you'll be able to amuse yourself.'

'It's my drama night,' she said, glad of it. 'I'll be out till elevenish.'

'High living. What are you doing?'

He wasn't really interested, she decided, just asking for the sake of it. She answered in like vein. 'Nothing you'd have heard of. What time are you planning on going home?'

'Whenever you're ready. You said something about some letters earlier. Urgent ones, I believe.'

They weren't, as it happened. She had mentioned them simply as a means of underlining her own position. Having said it at all, however, she could hardly now back down on the statement. She put down her cup and got up. 'About fifteen minutes, then.'

It was a relief to reach her own desk in the other office. She knew where she was here—and who. Adjusting to her new status was not going to be easy: worse in some ways than it had been as a child all those years ago. The only consolation—if it could be called that—was that this time she could meet Ross on more equal ground, at least so far as age was concerned. Strange how the same nine years could take on different dimensions. Six years ago it had been man and girl, now it was man and woman.

'Are we going to do those letters?' Kate Anthony asked from the desk across the room, jerking her back from introspection. There was a certain speculation in the other's regard. 'You said they should go tonight.'

And she knew as well as she did herself that they needn't, Kerry acknowledged ruefully. She liked Mrs Anthony and got along with her, despite the difference in their ages. One thing was certain, she was nobody's fool.

'I was holding my end up,' she admitted. 'But we may as well get them out anyway.'

'Mr Sinclair is very different from what I expected,' observed the secretary, poising pencil over notebook obligingly. 'I expect everyone is going to find it strange having such a young Chairman.'

Kerry opened her mouth to contradict that statement, then abruptly closed it again. Time enough to sort out the order of hierarchy. It was possible that the news of her own share in the estate had not yet filtered through, although it seemed unlikely. In conjunction with most business concerns, Sinclairs possessed a telegraph system that was second to none on the outside: a whisper started in the basement could be guaranteed to reach the top floor within a matter of minutes. But until someone else mentioned it, she would not. Let them consider she was staying on at Underwood on Ross's charity if they liked.

It wasn't until they were in the car on their way back to the house that he said calmly, 'I rang the cousins while you were dictating and arranged a board meeting for nine-thirty tomorrow. I'm seeing the market research guy at eleven, so you might set up a departmental managers' meeting for two o'clock.'

'Isn't that going over the GM's head?' Kerry asked, and received a quelling glance.

'He'll be presiding, naturally. I just want to make myself known.'

'Considering the way you avoided doing that this afternoon I'm surprised.'

'I didn't want any pomp and ceremony, that's why.'

Unlike Andrew who had revelled in trailing a retinue behind him on his regular monthly inspections of the Store, Kerry was bound to admit. Yet why not? It had been his only real vanity, and she could think of far worse ones.

It could have been her imagination that the house looked less welcoming this evening than it normally did. She still found it difficult to conceive that she actually owned half of it. Seen in retrospect, the conditions began to worry her more than a little. What would happen, for instance, if either of them wanted to get married at some point—or both, if it came to that? Would both couples be expected to occupy the same house for the extent of their lifetimes? Hardly an ideal situation.

'Drink?' Ross asked when they were inside.

Kerry shook her head. 'Too early for me, thanks, but you go ahead. Hope you won't mind an early dinner. I have to be at rehearsal for eight.'

'Give me a longer evening too,' he agreed. 'Need any help?'

'No, thanks, I did most of it this morning.' Briefly she wondered what he would have done had she taken advantage of his offer, and came to the conclusion that he probably wouldn't have turned a hair. Having lived in an apartment on his own—or one assumed it was on his own—he was no doubt perfectly accustomed to turning a hand to the culinary arts. For all she knew, he might even be a better cook than she was herself.

They ate at six-thirty, using the breakfast room at Ross's own suggestion as it saved time and trouble. He took his coffee with him to the study afterwards, saying he would see her later. Kerry had the feeling that he was glad to be alone again. Well, he wasn't on his own. Living with someone who was virtually a stranger was not going to be easy even if they did manage to keep things fairly amicable on the surface. Living with a man who attracted her physically into the bargain was going to be even more than difficult.

There was no sound from the study when she left the house at seven-thirty. She imagined the dark head bent industriously to the desk, the long, clever fingers moving swiftly and purposefully across the page as he transformed his rough notes into workable form. Ideas would be springing in that fertile brain, mind calculating the pros and cons like a computer. She felt a swift pang of regret that circumstances made their relationship so precarious. Had Andrew chosen to leave all his holdings in Sinclairs to his son she might not have agreed with everything he wanted to do to the place, but at least the responsibility for stopping him would not have been hers. This way they stood precious little chance of ever becoming friends.

Medfield Drama Group rehearsed each forthcoming production in a church hall close by the town centre one night a week, the latter increasing to two closer to the production date. Actual performances took place at the Civic Theatre over a Thursday, Friday and Saturday evenings twice a year, and usually played to a full house on all three nights. It helped, Kerry was bound to admit, being the only serious drama group in the town amidst an absolute glut of operatic societies, but they also had some very talented members. This time they were putting on Shaw's *Pygmalion*. With only a couple of relatively minor parts in previous productions to her credit, Kerry had been reluctant even to audition for Eliza, but several people had combined to persuade her. Surprised as she had been to be allotted the part, she was certainly enjoying doing it. They were sticking to the original script so far as possible, ignoring the tendency to update some of the playwright's more obscure humour. Properly interpreted, Larry Hall, their producer was fond of saying, no line should be beyond the scope of the average audience to appreciate. Kerry herself wasn't so sure about that, but along with the others she did her best.

She was almost the last to arrive. Larry detached himself from a group down by the platform which sufficed for a stage and came to meet her, rangy frame clad in his usual producer's outfit of faded jeans and shaggy sweater. At twenty-six, with an assured future ahead of him in his uncle's manufacturing firm, he was, Kerry sometimes reflected half humorously, just the kind of young man most mothers would like their daughters to marry. Not at all bad-looking, too, with his carefully casual blond hair and brilliant blue eyes. She knew he liked her, but so far she had been one among many. There was something different tonight in the way he looked at her.

'We weren't sure you'd be here,' he said. 'Word has it that stepbrother of yours is back in town?'

'Yes, he is.' Kerry wondered what other information had filtered through. 'Why should that be any reason to suppose I wouldn't be coming tonight?'

'Well, with the funeral only being yesterday and all that . . .'

'Life goes on,' she said, and was immediately ashamed of the implied flippancy in the retort. Leave that sort of thing to Ross. He could put it across without sounding anything more than down-to-earth. 'I mean, Andrew wouldn't have wanted me moping around the house,' she added swiftly. 'That sort of thing does nobody any good.'

The blue eyes held a curious expression. 'For a minute there I thought our Eliza had gone sour on us. It didn't sound a bit like you, Kerry.'

'No, I know. I've had a bit of a hard day.'

'Because of the stepbrother?'

'Partly.' More than that she was not prepared to say. 'Larry, about that bit of business you have me doing on Eliza's entrance at the start of the second act . . .'

As rehearsals went, this one tonight seemed, to Kerry at least, somewhat less than well directed. Larry appeared a little preoccupied, passing over moments which only a week ago would have had him tearing his hair at their inability to comprehend his meaning. With less than three weeks to go to the performance, they needed him more now than ever. One could only hope that whatever problem was occupying his mind would have been resolved by the following week.

Surprisingly, it was Larry who suggested that several of them go back to his flat for drinks and a chat after they had finished. Kerry accepted the invitation mainly because she was reluctant to return home and find Ross still up. It was a ridiculous attitude, she knew, considering that theirs was a permanent arrangement, and obviously one she was going to have to overcome, but for the present she was content to avoid as many private encounters as she conceivably could.

Larry's flat was roomy and well furnished. Kerry had not been there before but knew that at least a couple of the other female members of the group had—neither of whom, she noted, was here tonight. She refused alcohol on the grounds that she had to drive home, settling instead for coffee which she offered to make herself. Larry showed her where everything was in the small kitchenette and left her to it with the smiling remark that she looked quite at home there.

It was almost midnight before anyone made any move to leave. Kerry gathered together the used glasses and cups and quickly washed them up while Larry was chatting with 'Professor Higgins', alias Tom Cotteril, in the outer doorway. When she went back to the living room, Larry had just seen the latter off. He turned back from the door as she reached for her jacket.

'No tearing hurry, is there?' he asked pleasantly. 'There are one or two points I'd like to go over with you while we've the chance.'

Kerry hesitated, one arm half in her sleeve. 'It is rather late, Larry, and we both have to be up in the morning. Was it important?'

'Not vital. Just a couple of ideas I wanted to discuss. It won't take more than a few minutes to outline them. There's never much opportunity for individual discussion at normal rehearsal—at least, not enough.'

Kerry could go along with that. She had felt the lack pretty often these last few weeks. This was her first leading part and she wanted to make a success of it, for her own sake as well as the Company's. If Larry had some valid suggestion to make then the least she could do was listen. After all, it was late for him too. She let the jacket fall back on to the chair again.

'All right.'

They talked about Eliza for more than half an hour, by the end of which Kerry wasn't at all sure whether her grasp of the character had been improved on or detracted from. Larry was totally dedicated to the art of directing, there was no doubt about that, but she sometimes wondered if his techniques were a little too subtle for the average amateur drama group to interpret with any degree of success—or the average amateur audience either for that matter.

'It's been tremendously helpful,' she said in the end, 'but I really should go now.'

Larry laughed easily. 'Big brother waiting up for you?'

She sincerely hoped not. That would be too much. On the other hand, it was extremely doubtful that Ross would bother his head over her whereabouts. Why should he? She was hardly a child.

'It isn't that kind of relationship,' she said lightly. 'We just happen to occupy the same premises.'

His glance held sudden curiosity. 'On a permanent basis?'

'That was the condition.' She bit her lip, aware of having said more than she intended, and felt compelled to add, 'I suppose it could be divided into two without too much alteration.'

'You think that was what your stepfather intended?'

Kerry lifted her shoulders a little helplessly. 'I'm not sure just what he intended.'

'It seems pretty obvious to me,' Larry said, and she glanced at him in surprise.

'It does?'

'He planned on the two of you getting married, of course.'

That would hardly help matters, she was about to say before his meaning dawned on her. She felt her colour come up and quickly forced a laugh. 'Oh, come on! So far as Andrew was concerned, we were son and daughter!'

'But you weren't, were you?—his daughter, I mean. There's no blood tie between you and Ross. You're as free to marry him as anyone else.'

'Legally, perhaps, but there's more to it than that. Anyway, the question doesn't arise.'

'You don't fancy him that way?'

'No!' It occurred to her that her denial came out a little too forcefully for complete conviction. She made an attempt to amend any impression he might have gained. 'No, of course not. After six years I hardly know him. Besides ...'

The lift of his eyebrow was a prompt, but she had already said too much. The whole business of the Store was between her and Ross alone. 'I really must go,' she repeated. 'It's after twelve-thirty.'

Larry made no further attempt to detain her. 'I'll see you down to the car,' he offered. 'This time of night you never know who might be lurking about.'

She had parked the Allegro in a cul-de-sac around the corner along with the others on arrival. Now it stood alone under the street lamp. Larry took the key from her and inserted it in the lock, standing back with a flourish to allow her access to her seat and handing back the keys as she did so.

'They're showing *The Europeans* at the Odeon on Saturday,' he said. 'You mentioned it to Sandra last week. I'd like to see it too. How about going together?'

Gratified that he had remembered a casual remark, Kerry smiled her acceptance, 'I'd enjoy that.'

'My pleasure.' He closed the door, looking down at her with eyes turned an eerie shade by the overhead lighting as she wound down the window. 'No point in bringing your car into town. I'll pick you up at seven. We could have supper somewhere afterwards. All right?'

'Lovely.' She closed her mind to the thought that Ross might merit some consideration on his first Saturday night back in Medfield. This was more his home town than it was hers; there must be plenty of people he could call on.

On clear roads and such a fine, if cool night, it took her little more than fifteen minutes to reach Underwood. There was a light on in the hall, she noted as she drove up, but both drawing room and study were in darkness. From this side of the house she couldn't see Ross's room, but she assumed he had already gone up, leaving the light for the last comer as a matter of course.

As it was such a fine night she left the Allegro on the drive, letting herself into the house with her latchkey and closing the door gently behind her. The belt made a noise as she slid it along. For no earthly reason she found herself holding her breath as she listened for sound of movement upstairs. This was ridiculous. She was twenty-three, not thirteen! Even Andrew had given up monitoring her comings and goings once she reached eighteen or so.

She reached her own room without any indication from Ross, closing the door with a sense of relief. Tomorrow was another day—or should that be today, considering the time? No doubt she would eventually become accustomed to sharing the house with a man. After all, she had done it with Andrew for four years. She didn't need anyone to tell her how unrealistic that comparison was.

She was on the point of getting into bed some twenty minutes or so later when it occurred to her for the first time that Ross himself might have gone out too after he had finished his work. If that were so he was hardly going to be pleased to come home and find the door bolted against him.

Sighing, she reached for her light wrap and pulled it on, belting the waist tightly. Out on the landing she hesitated, looking down past the staircase to his door. Best to make certain, she supposed.

Her tentative tap brought no response. She tried again, then diffidently turned the handle to take a quick peep inside the room. It was in darkness, the bed so far as she could see untouched. That settled it. The door must remain unbolted until he saw fit to come in—that was if he ever did come in. Perhaps he had closer friends in Medfield than she had given him credit for.

Cynic, she chided herself as she made her way down to the hall again. That kind of observation was uncalled for. Because Ross had seen fit to kiss her last night there was no reason to imagine him a sex maniac. His motives in touching her at all went deeper than mere physical attraction—that was coincidental. What he had been showing her was contempt for their so-called relationship, warning her to expect no special consideration from him on the strength of it. Well, she didn't expect it. Neither would she want it. All she wanted from Ross was the right to be heard on an equal basis.

With the bolt unfastened, she found her eyes turning towards the study door, wondering if the report he had been working on was still in there. It seemed likely considering. The temptation to take a look was strong. After all, she would only be anticipating by a day or so, and she was going to need all the time at her disposal in order to consolidate her arguments.

The curtains were still drawn. Kerry switched on a light and crossed to the desk, swiftly scanning through the few papers lying on top. Not finding what she sought, she sat down in the swivel chair and began opening drawers, almost certain by now that the report had not been left in here yet reluctant to accept defeat until she had exhausted all possibilities.

The sudden pushing back of the half opened door took her completely by surprise, freezing her into an attitude of guilt with eyes gone wide and startled. Ross stood framed, clad in slacks and another of the silky sweaters, a folder in his hand.

'This what you're looking for?' he enquired sardonically. 'Sorry to disappoint you. I had it with me through in the sitting room.'

So that was why she had not seen any light downstairs, though Kerry wryly. The sitting room was at the rear of the house, the doorway around the bend of the hall beyond the staircase. Why he had been through there was immaterial. She supposed it was as good a place as any to sit.

'I thought you were out,' was all she could think of to say. 'Didn't you hear me come in?'

'Sure I heard you. At least, I heard the car—it woke me up. I lit the fire through there a couple of hours or so ago to read through what I've done so far. Must have dozed off.' He paused, studying her, expression hard to read. 'I guess it was a long rehearsal.'

'Some of us went back to our producers' place for drinks afterwards.' She registered the faint defensive note in her voice and could have kicked herself for it.

'I'm not complaining,' Ross returned maddeningly, also noting it. 'You're a big girl now. Who is your producer?'

'Larry Hall. I don't think you know him.'

'Isn't his family Hall Engineers?'

'That's his uncle. He works for him. Larry's parents emigrated to New Zealand a few years ago. He preferred to stay here.'

'As a surrogate son?'

'I suppose so. Old Mr Hall never had any children of his own.'

Ross was leaning against the jamb, effectively blocking her only means of exit from the room. 'That should make him a pretty good prospect as a husband.'

'I expect it does. I hadn't thought about it.'

'No?' The inflection was mocking. 'Doesn't marriage figure in your plans?'

'Certainly it *figures*,' borrowing his tone. 'With the right person.'

'And this Larry isn't?'

'I scarcely know him on a personal basis. This is the first time he's even asked me ...' She broke off, somehow reluctant to finish the sentence. Ross finished it for her.

'Asked you out? Understandable. Your position wasn't clarified until today. News get around fast in a place like this. It always did.'

Kerry got abruptly to her feet, closing the drawer she had been searching on his entry with unnecessary force. 'Larry isn't like that!'

'You said you scarcely knew him. How do you know *what* he's like?' He paused. 'Just as a matter of interest, if and when you do marry shall you be prepared to sell me back the controlling interest?'

Her head lifted. 'No,' she said firmly.

'That's what I thought.' He hadn't moved his position, but something about him seemed to have tautened. 'One point Dad forgot to cover.'

'If you're implying that I'd simply hand over my Sinclair stock to any man I did happen to marry, you're wrong.'

'Easy to say that now. Women are capable of anything when they're besotted enough with a man.'

She refused to rise to the taunt. 'So what solution do you suggest?'

'There's only one certain one.' The pause held deliberation. 'I could marry you myself.'

It was a moment before she could bring herself to reply. 'I've told you before I don't find that kind of joke funny,' she said stiffly.

'Who's joking? It was probably what Dad wanted anyway.'

That made two people within the space of a couple of hours who had said the same thing. Kerry tried to keep a rational viewpoint. 'If he'd wanted that he'd have made sure of it.'

'By making it a condition of the will, you mean?' Ross shook his head. 'Too unlikely to hold up under contention. Anyway, he was more subtle than that. I have to spring the noose myself.'

She stared at him, still unwilling to believe he could be serious. 'You really think I'd consent to marry you just to give you peace of mind over those lousy shares!'

'They're no way lousy shares,' he came back hardily. 'That's Sinclair stock, and it's staying right here in the family!'

'In the name of Rendal.' The anger exploding in her had some other emotion mingled with it. 'Ross, I wouldn't marry you for *any* reason, much less this one!'

'You won't marry anybody else. Not while you still hold that stock. I'll make sure of that.'

'How?'

The smile was without humour. 'Few men would want another man's leavings—not the kind you're likely to meet, at any rate. In a place like Medfield, the very fact that we're living alone together in this house is going to be a basis for gossip. You know how narrow-minded some quarters are.'

'I'd know it wasn't true—and so would anyone who cared about me.'

'Even if I swore it was?'

In that moment, and for the first time, Kerry knew what it was to really hate someone. He was capable—more than capable. 'You really are a prize louse, aren't you,' she said with bitterness.

'Through and through. You have the other alternative. Sell me the controlling interest.'

'You know I can't do that.'

'There's nothing to stop you, apart from a misguided loyalty.'

'To *your* father. Doesn't that mean anything?'

'My father,' he came back with irony, 'was all things to all people. You saw one side of him, I saw another.'

'You hated him, didn't you?'

'No, I didn't hate him.' Ross sounded suddenly weary. 'I objected to dancing to his tune, that's all.'

'Wouldn't you be doing that now if you married me just to get your hands on those shares?'

'No, because he wouldn't be here to control the merger. Anyway, you've sworn you won't contemplate marriage with me, so the question doesn't arise. If you won't sell me that stock either, that leaves me with no alternatives at all.'

'Except threats.' Her tone seared. 'They don't scare me, Ross.'

'All right then; we'll make it reality.'

She watched him put down the folder on the console table at the side of the door and start across the room towards her with the breath drying in her throat. Backing away was useless, there was nowhere to go.

'What are you trying to prove?' she said as he reached her.

'This,' he said, and pulled her up hard against him. His kiss was long, slow, searching, forcing her to open her lips to him despite herself. She felt him move backwards to rest his weight against the desk edge, drawing her with him and holding her there with the pressure of his hands on her spine. She was conscious wth every fibre of the muscular hardness of his body, the strength of his thighs locking hers. He moved a hand, unfastening the belt of her wrap to mould her breast in his cupped palm in a way which made her quiver.

'Don't,' she begged weakly when he moved his mouth from hers to kiss her jawline and down the length of her throat. 'Ross, no ...'

He laughed softly and mockingly and carried on, searing her skin like fire. Her wrap was half off her shoulders and she could do nothing to pull it back again. She fastened her hands in his hair, trying to pull back his head, but he ignored the pain, drawing a gasp from her as his lips found their mark.

Nothing in her experience had prepared her for quite such depth of sensation; for the swift aching need rising in her. Without realising it, she found her hands had stopped yanking back his head and were now holding it closer to her, her fingers curling into the crisp darkness of his hair. This time when she murmured his name it had a different sound, a different kind of pleading.

When he lifted her up into his arms she made no move to resist, burying her face in his shoulder.

'Not here,' he said on a rough note. 'Your room or mine?'

If he hadn't spoken; if he'd simply carried her upstairs and laid her on the bed she would have given herself to him without hesitation. The sound of his voice broke the spell for her, bringing her back to face the full realisation of what she was doing.

'Oh God,' she muttered. 'Put me down! Put me down, Ross!'

He looked down at her, muscle jerking visibly at the corner of his mouth. 'Just like that? What do you think I'm made of?'

'I'm sorry, I shouldn't have let it go that far.' Distress made her voice shake. 'You shouldn't have started it. I—I couldn't stop you.'

'You didn't want to stop me. Not hard enough to put any real effort into it.' His mouth was set. 'Why should I stop now?'

'Because I'm asking you to—begging you to, if you like.' She was desperate, aware that emotions once aroused could quite as easily be aroused again. Tonight was one thing, tomorrow quite another. She wanted to be able to meet her own eyes in the mirror without cringing with shame at the memory of how easy he had found her. 'I . . . can't.'

Eyes narrowed, he searched her face for a long tense moment, then abruptly lowered her to the ground again, turning back to the desk to open the onyx cigarette box. The table lighter flared, and was extinguished with a hard movement of his thumb, the inhalation of his breath on smoke clearly audible. When he turned back to her he was in control of himself, taut and steely.

'You'd better get to bed,' he said.

'Not until I've made you understand.'

His brows lifted. 'Understand what?'

'Why I acted the way I did just now.'

'That hardly needs any explanation, does it? It's perfectly simple. You wanted what I wanted, only you changed your mind. It's a female trait to wait till she's got a man fairly and squarely landed, then kick him where it hurts.

This time you got away with it. Next time you might not be so lucky.'

'It wasn't like that,' she protested. 'It really wasn't.'

'I said go to bed.'

She stared at him helplessly, reluctant to go yet knowing it useless to stay. 'Can't we start again?' she asked pleadingly. 'From the beginning, I mean. I can't sell out your father's trust in me, but I'll try to see your point of view with regard to the Store wherever I possibly can.'

'Including self-service?' he enquired sardonically. 'That's the only viable proposition.'

Kerry bit her lip. 'You know I can't go along with that.'

'Can't or won't?'

'Both. It's the one thing Andrew would have wanted to hold on to. Without its service Sinclairs is dead.'

'It's dead now. Dead and dusty. There's a whole generation out there who couldn't care less about personal service.'

'So what would you plan on doing, sacking half the staff?'

'They'd be utilised in other ways. You'll see how when you read my report.'

'I don't want to read your damned report!' The emotions of a moment ago were submerged by those rising in her now. 'I don't want to know what your plans are because they're not going ahead! Not on those lines.'

Ross eyed her consideringly through the smoke curling up from the end of his cigarette. 'If I get the cousins on my side that gives me a sixty per cent vote.'

'They won't, not without my agreement. Do you imagine they won't realise why Andrew split his stock?'

'There's going to be a lot of money involved. Do *you* imagine they couldn't find a use for extra income?'

'Not at the cost of everything the name of Sinclairs stands for. They're your father's generation too, remember.

They have values you wouldn't even know how to recognise.'

'But you can.'

'Yes, I can. There's plenty you can do to improve profit without going that far.'

His lips twisted. 'Maybe you'd better take over reorganisation yourself if you're so hot on ideas.'

'I'm not trying to take over. I'll go along with just about anything except self-service.'

'You'll go along with that too because you're going to have to eventually. Unless you'd rather lose Underwood?'

'That wasn't what Mr Watling said.'

'It's what he was intimating. CTT on an estate the size of this one is going to run into pretty big figures, with a subsequent reduction in other income after selling out stock to meet it. Dad must have realised himself that there was going to have to be some adjustment made after his death.'

'Of course he realised. He would have calculated just how much was going to be needed too.'

'Four years ago. Things are different now.' Intolerance curled his mouth. 'Grow up, sweetheart. Stop living in the past.'

'It's a sight better than the present.' Kerry looked at him with resignation, recognising the sheer hopelessness of trying to convince him. If figures eventually proved that Underwood was at risk then she might have to sacrifice more of Andrew's principles than she wished, but until it was proved she was hanging on. 'Goodnight, Ross.'

'Kerry.' His voice stopped her halfway across the room to the door, quiet but forceful. 'I meant what I said a while back. You show any signs at all of getting interested in another man and I'll break it up.'

She didn't turn round. 'You can try,' she said.

CHAPTER FOUR

THE report took a week to complete. Handing out copies at the second full board meeting on the Thursday morning, Ross apologised for the delay.

'There's more involved than even I imagined first hand,' he added. 'I'd suggest you all read it through before we get down to any kind of discussion.'

'My eyes aren't what they were,' complained John Barratt. 'Can't you just give us the gist of it?'

'The gist is that we need to restructure the whole organisation from top to bottom to get anywhere worthwhile. Some of it can be done gradually, much of it's imperative. Stock control, for instance. There's too much cash tied up there.'

'Always in stock at Sinclairs,' quoted James in the manner of one producing an undefeatable argument. 'A customer turned away is a customer lost!'

'With an efficient reordering system there's no need for vast amounts of stock to be carried.'

'Isn't it up to the individual department buyers to decide on their own needs?'

'That's part of the trouble, there's too much individuality. One of the first things needed is an overall merchandise manager to supervise purchasing and produce a proper budgetary control system. Take furs, as a case in point. I calculate we have some seventeen thousand pounds lying fallow, a lot of it in relatively old stock.' His eyes met Kerry's. 'Any questions?'

'Yes,' she said. 'When are you going back to Detroit?'

'My dear girl!' James sounded more than a little shocked. 'That's hardly a nice way to talk.'

Her expression was bland. 'Sorry if it sounded that way. I was only asking because I assume you will have to go back to sort things out over there.'

Ross answered coolly. 'You're quite right, I will. I plan on leaving tonight, which is why I'm in a hurry to get some decisions made.'

'How long will you be gone?'

'Hard to say. My contract calls for a month's notice, but I may be able to make arrangements.'

James said, 'You're not on the board?'

He smiled. 'It's a family run group. I attend board meetings, of course, but I'm not allowed to buy stock. Which brings me to another point. The present GM is due for retirement in approximately eleven months' time. In view of the advantages of having top management on the board, I think we should make his successor a director.'

'Appointed from within?' Kerry asked, already suspecting the answer.

She got it with cool precision. 'Not if I can help it. Promotion isn't a right, it has to be merited. Not one of the upper management is suited to any higher position. Some of them can't even handle what they've got. It's a pity we can't lower compulsory retirement age to sixty and clear out the dead wood in one fell swoop. They've been with the firm too long to adjust satisfactorily.'

'That depends on how far the adjustment goes.' The challenge was in both eyes and voice. 'I suppose you already have a successor for the GM in mind.'

'Hardly yet. We've almost a year to find him.'

'Does it have to be a man?'

His smile cut. 'Fancy the job yourself?'

'That wasn't what I meant.'

'I'm relieved. Liberalisation is the last thing we need.

Yes, it probably will be a man, if only for the reason that good female executive material is relatively rare.'

Kerry had asked for it and she had got it, right in the teeth. Considering the last few days, she should have known better than to leave herself that far open, she reflected wryly. Unarmed combat was the best way of describing their relationship: Ross certainly needed no extra arms; he had a very threatening pair ready attached. Not that he'd attempted to use them on her since, relying instead on the razor edge of his tongue to put her down.

James Barratt looked slyly approving of the chastisement she had received. Kerry doubted if he actively disliked her as a person, but he belonged to a school where women knew their place and stayed in it. Only a few weeks ago he had told Andrew she had too much to say for herself. Andrew had laughed in the retelling and tousled her hair the way he used to when she was younger. 'My compensation,' he had said. Remembering the moment now, she wondered why she failed to appreciate the significance of the term then. From her he had gained the loyalty and adulation he had failed to receive from his son. What she said was only what he had taught her to say. His mouthpiece. Well, there was nothing wrong in that. She had believed in him; she still did. And his son was not about to rob her of that belief.

'You'll be taking the chair, of course,' James was saying now, bringing her attention sharply back to present proceedings. 'I don't think we need to bother with any vote.'

'I'm willing,' Ross agreed equably, and lifted an eyebrow in Kerry's direction.

Looking from James to John, then back to Ross, she acknowledged the waste of time and effort in objection. Certainly the cousins were not going to vote her into the chair. To be honest, she didn't really want it. Under the circumstances, the power it allotted was nominal.

'It's all yours,' she said.

'Thanks.'

'Don't mention it.'

His glance held intolerance. 'If you're really intent on having the last word make it constructive, will you? We're none of us here to play games.'

She flushed, knowing she deserved that too, and wisely stayed silent. When it came to verbal confrontation he had her beaten hands down every time. She didn't know why she kept on trying.

'We'll be running the customer questionnaire scheme from Saturday on through the following week,' he went on. 'That should give us a good average coverage. It's going to take some time to collate the findings, but if they run true to form we should find two or three ideas worth looking into. By the time I get back we'll need to be ready to start putting plans into operation.'

When he got back. For the first time it occurred to Kerry to think about what he was giving up over there. In six years he must have formed friendships, to say nothing of his home and his work. How would he feel when he returned to that life-style? Would he have regrets? If he did, she decided, he wouldn't allow them to get in the way. He had what he wanted here—what he had always wanted.

Being alone in the house again was going to feel strange. Yet how welcome the change would be. Perhaps she had been taking things too far in phoning Larry last Saturday afternoon and cancelling their arrangement, but at the time Ross's threat had been too fresh in her mind to risk ignoring. It hadn't put Larry off, at any rate. He had asked her out again at rehearsal last night. And this time she was going to go, Ross or no Ross.

They closed the meeting on the understanding that the next one would take place on his return. Carrying their copies of the report, the cousins left. Ross caught Kerry's eye as she was about to follow their example and nodded brusquely towards the chair she had just vacated.

'Sit down,' he said. 'There are one or two things I want to say to you.'

She looked at him for a moment, then shrugged and complied. 'So get it off your chest.'

'That's one of them,' he came back grimly. 'Look, Kerry, when we're back at the house you can get at me any way you want, but do it here again in front of others and I'm going to lose my rag with you.'

'Why?' she asked recklessly. 'Does it attack your precious dignity?'

'I'll attack yours in a minute,' he threatened. 'You might benefit from a damned good hiding!' He saw the change of expression in her eyes and smiled grimly. 'Don't think you're beyond it.'

'I'm sure *you're* not,' she retorted with what coolness she could muster.

'Fine. So stop needling me. Like it or not, we have to work together.' He paused, tone altering a little. 'Spend some time over that report, will you? I've quoted facts and figures to back up my recommendations.'

'They're rather more than recommendations, aren't they?' she said low-toned. 'You want to make a clean sweep.'

'Not all at once. Some of it will have to happen gradually. Staff retraining will take some time. You'll see I've made provision for a special release scheme for juniors. They're the ones we're going to be drawing our new management from eventually, and simply following the methods of their present superiors isn't going to be enough.'

'It means a lot of adaptation.'

'Yes, it does.'

'What about those who prove unequal to it?'

His jaw firmed. 'We'll cross that particular bridge when

we come to it. You'll have at least a couple of weeks to sort out your priorities before I get back.'

She looked at him for a moment. 'You really think they'll be ready to let you go that quickly?'

'Under the circumstances, I'm hoping so. My next in line is well qualified to step into my shoes overnight if needs be.'

She said softly, 'I suppose all your managing staff are male.'

'No, they're not. I said the female was relatively rare, not impossible to find. My merchandise manager is a woman, and right on top of her job—she wouldn't be in it if she weren't.'

'Young?'

'Twenty-eight.' There was irony in his glance. 'And to save any further questions, she's blonde, blue-eyed, very good-looking—and no, she didn't get the job by utilising those assets.'

'You just noticed in passing.'

'I'd have to be blind not to. There's one thing I learned very early on, and that was to keep business and pleasure strictly separate. It makes for a very much better working relationship. Take you and me, for instance. One thing gets in the way of the other. Think how much easier life would be if you weren't so involved in Sinclairs.'

'I don't see what difference it would make.' Her tone was flat. 'We'd still hate the sight of one another.'

His smile was faint. 'Is that what we do?'

'What would you call it?' she challenged, and saw the grey eyes take on a sudden glint.

'Come over here and I'll show you what I call it.'

She gazed at him without moving, seeing the strong line of his jaw, the easy relaxed stance, hands resting lightly on the back of the chair in front of him, remembering the feel of those same hands on her skin, the touch of his lips. A part of her wanted badly to obey the invitation, to get up and go to him and have him take her in his arms again the way he had done the other night. There was no denying the attraction he had for her. It had always been there from the time she had been old enough to recognise the symptoms for what they were. It had lain dormant in her all the years of his absence, ruining other relationships because there had never been anyone else to compare with Ross. And now he was back and the yearning was still there, only different now, intensified to almost unbearable proportions. She had a sudden longing to give in here and now, to tell him he could do as he liked with the Store—and with her. She loved him and she wanted him, any way she could have him, but her debt to his father made it all so impossible.

'Kerry?' His tone had altered, the mockery replaced by something deeper, more intimate. He straightened up slowly from the chair back, his eyes not leaving her face. 'If you won't come to me,' he said, 'I guess I'll have to come to you.'

'No, Ross!' She put out her hands in front of her to fend off his advance, eyes darkening. 'I don't want you touching me again!'

'You do. As badly as I want to touch you.' He pulled her to her feet, holding her there in front of him with his fingers hard on her upper arms. 'If it weren't for this damned business we'd be free to please ourselves—make our own decisions.' One hand came up to touch her face, smoothing the line of her cheek in a way that made her quiver. 'I want to make love to you, Kerry. I wanted it the other night, and so did you. Only it's impossible for us to develop any kind of real relationship while we're caught up in this mess Dad left us with. You know that, don't you?'

'Yes.' Her voice was low and husky. 'I know.'

'Then do the sensible thing and stop fighting me.'

'I ... can't. He trusted me.'

'Of course he did. But he was wrong to put you in this position. The old order of things died with him; it's time to start over again now, and that means totally. We can't afford to indulge an out-moded concept any more. Sinclairs has to more than pay its way.' The hand steadied under her chin, lifting her mouth to his and holding it there while he kissed her with slowly mounting passion, making her respond to him by sheer force of will. When he finally lifted his head again he was smiling, his hands tender. 'I remember once catching a glimpse of you nude when you were about fifteen,' he said. 'You were just starting to develop a woman's body then—beautiful little breasts, like apples. They're fuller now, but just as firm. Irresistible!'

'Ross ...' she was tremulous, wanting his touch with everything in her, yet mindful of where they were ... 'someone might come in.'

'We could always lock the door.'

'No.' She caught at his hand, pushing it away, rebuttoning her blouse without being able to bring herself to meet his eyes. 'I—I can't think straight when you do that.'

He laughed, and put her hand to his lips, his other arm holding her to him. 'You're such a mixture, Kerry. You respond so marvellously, yet you're so reluctant to really let yourself go. You're still a virgin, aren't you?'

She bridled a little, sensing ridicule. 'Is there anything so wrong in that?'

'No, not a bit. I like the thought. You know, there's a whole lot of rubbish talked about today's permissive society and how a girl has as much right to premarital sex as a man, but selfish or not, most men would like to think they were first and last with the girl they marry.' He caught the quality in her sudden stillness and looked at her. 'Do you think marriage would be such a bad idea?'

'Just to keep the stock in the name of Sinclair?' Her voice sounded thick.

He pulled a wry face. 'That was a rotten way of putting it, I admit. I wanted to shake you up. No, forget the stock for the moment. I'm talking about us. It's probably too soon to be sure, but on the face of it we'd seem to have what it takes.'

'There's more to marriage than sex,' she protested.

'I imagine there is,' he agreed tolerantly. 'But don't try telling me sex isn't important to you because I'm not going to believe you.' He paused, searching her face with a look which brought the warmth to her cheeks. 'I wish I weren't going tonight.'

'I'm glad you are.' She tried to sound convincing about it. 'You undermine all my better principles.'

'Including the one we've been doing all the fighting over?'

'Yes,' she admitted with a resigned sigh. 'Even that. I don't want to fight you, Ross.'

'You won't have to now. Not over anything. Just trust my judgment, darling. Believe me, I know what I'm talking about.' He kissed her again, lightly this time, and put her away from him with an obvious reluctance. 'You're right, this is neither the time nor place. We'll have to make plans as soon as I get back.'

Kerry was cautious, still not wholly able to believe that he meant what he had said. 'So soon?'

'Why not? What is there to wait for?'

'Love,' she wanted to say, but couldn't force the word out. Perhaps, manlike, he was taking it as said—except that nothing he had said so far indicated quite that depth of emotion. So all right, she told herself stoutly, he didn't yet love her the way she wanted him to, but that wasn't to say he wouldn't in time. At least she had a basis to work on.

'Why didn't you tell me you were leaving tonight?' she

murmured, avoiding the question. 'Was it such a sudden decision?'

'No, not really. The opportunity just never seemed right these last few days.' He moved away from her to start putting papers back into his briefcase. 'The mood you've been in, I thought you might be too glad to get rid of me.'

'Any mood I was in you put me in,' she said. 'You've acted all week as if all you wanted to do was take a swing at me.'

His mouth widened briefly. 'Sheer frustration. If you can't join 'em beat 'em!'

'Now you're being satirical.'

'No, I'm not—or at least, if I am, it's at my own expense.' He closed the briefcase with a decisive snap of the lock, and looked at her. 'I'll miss the provocation these next couple of weeks.'

She said shakily, 'I wish I was coming with you,' and saw the grey eyes flicker.

'So do I, but it wouldn't be practical. I'm going to be pretty tied up. I'll take you over some time in the not too distant future and show you what I've been talking about.'

'And check up on your successor at the same time?' she teased.

Ross laughed. 'There could be something in that. I can see I'm going to have to watch it with you or I won't have a motive to call my own.'

Kerry doubted that. No matter how well one got to know Ross Sinclair there would probably always be a part of him he kept to himself. That was how it should be. No one should bare themselves heart and soul to another. It left no reserve.

'It's just gone half past three,' he said now, glancing at the boardroom clock. 'My flight isn't until nine, so that gives me a good five hours to get back to the house, pick up my things and make Ringwood for eight-thirty. I'll have a meal on the way.' His eyes slid over her face and dropped to the recently refastened blouse, his lips curving. 'Come on back with me, Kerry. To Underwood, I mean.'

The temptation to say yes was strong, but some element of caution held her back. 'I don't think that's such a good idea,' she said.

The resignation in his shrug was good-humoured enough. 'Maybe you're right. I could finish up missing my flight. Something to look forward to when I get back.'

Kerry hesitated, searching the strong features without finding what she sought. 'Ross ...'

'Don't worry,' he said on a gentler note, accurately interpreting her expression. 'I shan't be expecting anything you're not prepared to give. You're entitled to a traditional wedding night if that's what you want.' It was his turn to hesitate, though only for a second or two. 'You won't be wanting a big wedding with all the trimmings, will you? After all, there isn't much family left.'

'No, of course not.' She bit her lip, hardly knowing how to put what she wanted to say. 'Ross, don't you think you're being ... well, too hasty, I suppose?'

'About marrying you?' He dropped the briefcase back on the desk and drew her to him again, holding her close with his face against her cheek for a moment. 'How much convincing do I have to do? I *want* to marry you, Kerry. Do you want to marry me?'

'Well ... yes.'

'You don't sound very sure.'

'It's not that. I don't want you to regret it, that's all.'

'I'm not going to regret it. Neither are you. Remember, it's what Dad would have wanted too.'

She pulled away from him a little, just far enough to see his face. 'How can you be sure of that?'

'Because I knew him. Better than you give me credit for.' There was a certain tension in the set of his mouth, relaxing even as she registered it. 'He probably always hoped this would happen. Even when you were only sixteen he was singing your praises to me constantly.'

She wrinkled her nose. 'That must have really got to you.'

'It sure did. I could see for myself you were growing into a lovely young thing without having the fact pushed down my throat several times a day. If I got nasty with you at times it was only in sheer self-defence.'

Kerry smiled, remembering. 'Sometimes you were unbearable. I used to wish all kinds of horrible afflictions on you.'

'But not any more?' softly.

'No. Not right now, at any rate.'

'Meaning there could be a time when malevolence might return?' He sounded amused. 'I'll have to watch out.' He took another look at the clock over her shoulder and sighed. 'Honey, I'm going to have to go—I haven't packed yet. You're going to be okay on your own in the house?'

'Of course.' She resisted the urge to cling, returning his kiss with some element of restraint still remaining. 'Take care of yourself, Ross.'

'I will.' He kissed her again, fleetingly this time, and let her go. 'See you in a couple of weeks.'

She stayed where she was for several moments after he had gone, trying to sort out her emotions. Less than half an hour ago they had been at loggerheads, and now here they were practically engaged to be married. It had all happened too quickly—given her no time to think. Not that she wasn't going to have plenty of that during the coming couple of weeks or so while Ross was away. In that sense his absence was a good thing. It gave them both time to reconsider. No matter how much Ross denied it, her Sinclair stock had to have some bearing on his desire to change her name to his, and that wasn't the ideal basis for a marriage.

She got home at six-thirty to an empty and lonely house, ate a hurriedly prepared and not very substantial meal in the kitchen and took her copy of the report through to the study with a pot of coffee. It had been cool enough all day for Mrs Payne to have switched on the central heating. Kerry turned up the room stat a point and sat down in one of the big leather club chairs to start reading.

She did it twice in all, first quickly to assimilate the basic facts, then more slowly, dwelling on individual points. The amount of detail amazed her, not only in the tearing down of present techniques but also in the building up of new. And it all jelled—at least it did on paper. One could almost see the new Sinclairs rising like a phoenix from the ashes of the old. Not an overnight rebirth, of course. It would take time both to re-equip and to retrain. The projected plans for the change-over to self-service brought a return of the doubts she had cast away in Ross's arms. If he had his way there would be nothing left but featureless efficiency. Could she so far reject Andrew's claim on her loyalty, knowing full well what he had intended her to do?

It would have been difficult to break her date with Larry Hall again without going into explanations she preferred not to make as yet, so Kerry kept to the arrangement. The film they had both wanted to see was still showing, and enabled her to forget her problems for the space of a couple of hours or so.

It was Larry who suggested supper after the film, taking her to a small French restaurant off the town centre which Kerry had not even known existed.

'They do the most delicious onion soup in the proper French style,' he said. 'The chef is only young, but he apparently spent a couple of years working over there before going into partnership to open this place. You'll like it.'

Kerry did. The atmosphere was as close to a genuine bistro as it was possible to get outside the country itself the food every bit as good as Larry had made out. He insisted on having wine to go with the meal, although Kerry would have rather not.

'It's something of a celebration,' he said. 'Our first date The first of many, I hope.'

She should have told him then, but something held her back. Those moments in the boardroom three days ago had taken on a certain quality of unreality. There had been no word from Ross, not even to tell her of his safe arrival. Not that there was much doubt, of course. In the case of travellers, no news was normally good news. But surely a phone call would not have taken up so much of his time.

'Do you really think we're going to be ready for the show less than a fortnight?' she asked, evading the issue.

'What you really mean is, are *you* going to be ready,' he said smilingly. 'Yes, of course you are. Your cockney accent needs a bit more concentration, perhaps, but otherwise you're all set to be a hit.'

Kerry laughed. 'Surprising how difficult it is to drop aitches in the right places and put them in where they don't belong. Like learning a whole new language. I really did mean the show as a whole, though. Last night was a shambles.'

'Hey!' he protested. 'As the man in charge, I resent that remark!' He laughed too then, and shrugged wryly. 'Sometimes you get those nights when nothing goes right. It's happened before, no doubt it will again. But you'd better be on your toes come Tuesday's rehearsal or heads will roll!'

'You sound like Henry the Eighth,' she quipped, and drew a mock glare.

'Thou dares to taunt me, woman!'

'Only in jest, sire.' She met his eyes and grinned back,

liking him in this mood. 'How about doing an historical some time?'

'We'll put it to the vote.' There was something unfathomable in his gaze. 'We should have done this before, Kerry. Why haven't we?'

'Because you never asked me,' she replied lightly. 'As a matter of fact, I thought you were rather heavily involved with Heather Wyatt.'

'Involved is the wrong word,' he came back smoothly. 'We went around together for a while, that's all. Heather isn't the type I'd want to get really serious about. When it comes to thinking about settling down a man becomes ... well, choosy, I suppose. He wants a girl with intellect as well as looks. Someone he can respect, and trust not to let him down. Girls like that are choosy too, of course. They have a right to be.'

He could afford to say that, knowing he would naturally be an obvious choice, Kerry reflected, and was immediately ashamed. Cynicism was coming too easily these days. She had to stop it.

Conversation became general after that. Only when Larry finally brought the car to a halt in front of the house did he attempt to return to more personal matters again.

'You're a terrific person, Kerry,' he said softly. 'I've enjoyed tonight tremendously. We're going to be pretty busy this next week and a half with the play, I know, but let's do it again afterwards?' He took her answer for granted, leaning over to kiss her in a light and friendly fashion on the cheek. 'I won't come in, considering the time.' The pause was brief. 'By the way, did you hear from that stepbrother of yours yet?'

She shook her head, expression controlled. 'I expect he's busy. Winding up a job like he had must take some doing.'

'But the rewards make it worthwhile. There's a strong rumour going round that he intends replanning the whole store from top to bottom. Not before time, if I might say so. It's a bit antiquated.'

'Not so much so,' she protested, 'or it wouldn't be in existence.'

'Yes, but there's a vast difference between what it is and what it could be. Pity your stepfather never saw the potential.'

'He did, and rejected it.'

'Then he was very short-sighted. Even in Medfield we have to move with the times.' He studied her profile for a moment before adding on an odd note, 'You're not considering blocking him in any way, are you?'

So he was aware of her position with regard to Sinclairs. Kerry wasn't sure why she should feel so depressed by that realisation.

'I'm not considering anything at the moment, except sleep,' she said, striving for a suitably light note. 'It is late, Larry, as you said.'

'Of course.' He watched her get out of the car. 'You're not scared on your own in this big place?'

'No.' She very easily could become so, though, she reflected dryly, if people didn't stop suggesting the idea to her. She added, 'Andrew was very security conscious. There are special locks on all the windows and doors, and an alarm system connected direct to the station.'

'Good. I'd hate to think of anything happening to you. Go on in and wave to me from your bedroom window to say all's well.'

'I can't, it's on the other side of the house.' She closed the car door and moved towards the house, turning on the step to lift a hand in brief farewell. 'Goodnight, Larry.'

He stayed put until she was inside, then started the engine and drove away. Listening to him go, Kerry regretted not having made her position clearer. Yet was it so clear even to her? she wondered. Ross had asked her to marry him, true, but was she going to do so? She wasn't even certain of the quality of her own emotions any more, much less his.

She was just emerging from the bathroom when the telephone rang. Her first thought was Ross, although she should have known that he would take account of the time difference between here and the States. She ran to the extension in her bedroom, lifting the receiver with a breathlessness which belied her recent doubts.

'Yes?'

'Am I speaking to Kerry Rendal?' asked a female voice with an accent she did not immediately recognise.

'Yes,' Kerry said again in some surprise. 'Who is that, please?'

'You won't know me. I doubt if Ross will have mentioned my name.' The inflection was bitter. 'I thought you should know before you marry him what kind of man he is. How would you feel about a man who lives with a woman for six months and then turns her out on the street?'

Something froze deep down inside Kerry. 'Who *are* you?' she demanded. 'What are you talking about?'

'My name is Margot—Margot Kilkerry. Ask Ross about me and see the guilt in his face!'

'I don't believe you.' Kerry's voice was shaky, her face white. 'You're making this up!'

'I can't make up facts. His address was mine until a few days ago. He told me to go when he got back here, just like that. We were going to be married before his father died. He was with me on vacation when the news came through.'

Kerry took a grip on herself. 'How did you know where to contact me?'

'I knew the name of the house and the town. The International operator did the rest. That really isn't important, is it? I did reach you.'

'What do you expect me to do?' It was little more than a whisper.

'That's up to you. I can't force you to give him up, but you should know the truth.'

'If I give him up he'll still be leaving Detroit.'

'Because of the inheritance he shares with you? Yes, he told me about that. If you'd give him the control which should be his by rights, there wouldn't be any need for him to marry you at all. You have so much already, why want a man who doesn't love you? He'd bring me over there if it weren't for you. You just think about that.'

Kerry heard the click of the receiver being replaced thousands of miles away, but made no immediate move to replace her own, holding it cradled numbly against her cheek. There could be no questioning the validity of this woman's claim; her voice had rung with conviction. Ross had obviously told her everything, including his true reasons for marrying her, Kerry. The calculation hurt most of all. How could he do this to her—to Margot either? What kind of man indeed!

How long she sat there on the edge of the bed after finally putting down the phone she couldn't have said. Her thoughts were incoherent. The urge to get in touch with Ross grew slowly but inexorably in her. What good it could do she had no idea, but she had to speak to him, to tell him what she thought of him, to express her contempt and bitterness while it still rode high and wild inside her.

The book where she had found his address the morning after his father's death was downstairs in the study still. She found it at the back of the top drawer, and laid it open at the appropriate page on the desk in front of her as she reached for the phone.

It took a few minutes to obtain the information she required. As she had thought, she could dial STD right through from here. It was a long number and she had to have two attempts before she got it right. She heard the series of clicks denoting the various relay pick-ups, a lengthy pause and then, surprisingly clear, the ringing tone at the far distant end of the line.

Ross answered so promptly he must have been standing right beside the instrument when it rang. 'Sinclair,' he said.

Now that the moment was on her, Kerry found her mouth and throat had lost all moisture. She swallowed painfully and managed to force her voice out. 'It's Kerry.'

'Kerry?' He sounded startled. 'It must be two o'clock in the morning over there! Where the devil have you been? I was trying to contact you earlier for more than three hours.'

'I went to the cinema,' she said truthfully, and paused. 'Why were you ringing me, Ross?'

'Why do you think? I wanted to speak to you. Sorry I didn't do it before this, but things have been a bit hectic.' There was an odd note in his voice. 'Kerry, are you okay? You sound strange.'

'Yes, I'm fine. It must be the line.' The words were forming themselves. 'Do you have any idea yet how long it's going to be?'

'Not exactly. One or two problems have cropped up—nothing serious, though. With any luck I'll be away by the middle of the month.' His tone altered again, taking on a more intimate note. 'I miss you, Kerry.'

'I miss you too.' It hurt to say it.

'Everything all right at the Store?'

'Yes.' She was on firmer ground now. This was where his real interest lay. 'We started the customer questionnaire this morning as scheduled. Apparently the response has been good today. Oh, and there've been several enquiries regarding leased floor space. I didn't realise you'd got as far as that.'

'Just a few feelers I put out. Doesn't do any harm to arouse interest.'

No, she thought with bitterness, it doesn't. Suddenly she could bear no more. 'I must go now, Ross,' she said. 'It's awfully late.'

'Yes, I know. You should be in bed.' The smile was there. 'I wish I was with you. Goodnight, honey. I'll be in touch.'

Kerry carefully replaced the receiver and stood for a moment looking at it. Coward, she thought. You're nothing but a coward! She had stood here talking to Ross as if nothing at all had happened. It was too late now to make accusations over the phone. She would have to wait until he returned here to Underwood and face him with the whole affair direct to his face. But how was she to get through the time between?

CHAPTER FIVE

The play had a good first night, a better second, and finished its three-day run on a blazing note of success which left the whole cast in a state of euphoria.

'Of course, Kerry's the real heroine of the evening,' Tom Cotteril exclaimed generously at the celebration party after the final performance. 'Talk about pulling out all the stops! You were marvellous, girl, bloody marvellous!'

Others chimed in, making Kerry flush with a mixture of pleasure and embarrassment. From his seat at her side, Larry put a faintly possessive arm about her shoulders and grinned his approval.

'Too true. You turned in a brilliant performance. Better, even, than anybody anticipated. What happened to you this last week or so? You showed promise before, but not to the same extent.'

'I expect I only started to get my teeth into the role towards the end,' Kerry said, accepting the praise because there was no other way. She wondered what they would all say if she told them the truth; that her total immersion in the role of Eliza had been her only means of putting other matters out of her mind. Now the play was over and so was her escape. But not immediately. Not tonight. That was why she had invited the cast back here to Underwood for the party. Tomorrow she could start planning her strategy for when Ross returned home. Tonight she didn't want to think about him.

Somebody put a new record on the turntable and turned out a couple of lights to suit the mood of the music better. Larry said softly, 'Let's dance, Kerry.'

She didn't object when he held her close. She needed

someone to lean on. Larry had been good for her these last weeks; they had shared a common interest. Whatever his initial motivation in asking her out, she felt that he wanted to be with her now for herself as much as any other reason.

'I'm proud of you,' he murmured against her hair. 'My lovely, clever Kerry. We've wasted a lot of time, you and I, but we're going to make up for it now, aren't we?'

'If you want to,' she said, and he laughed.

'You bet I want to! We'll have a good time together—get to know one another properly. We've a lot in common to start with. We even look good together, don't you think?'

She twisted her head a little to catch a glimpse of the two of them in the mirror by the door as they moved past, and felt a swift pang run through her at the sight of his fair head against her own coppery one.

'Yes,' she said, 'we do, don't we?'

He was kissing her when Ross walked in. Kerry sensed the sudden change of atmosphere in the room, and broke away from the light embrace, seeing her stepbrother standing in the doorway with a feeling of time reversed. There was no expression on his face at all, but his eyes were steely.

'Celebrating something?' he asked into the temporary silence. His smile looked normal enough on the surface; probably only Kerry of all those in the room was aware of the tautness behind it. 'I guess the play was a hit?'

Somehow Kerry forced herself to take over, to perform introductions and act naturally. A couple of the older members already knew him from previous days, greeting him with obvious speculation but no apparent censure. Without effort, he became one of the party, getting himself a drink and responding pleasantly to conversational overtures, treating Kerry to no more than the occasional glance over the following hour or so, and those revealing little of what was going on inside the dark head.

'Shall you be staying in England for good now?' asked one of the girls sitting close by him at one point with some light of self-interest in her eyes. 'No commuting backwards and forwards across the Atlantic?'

'No commuting,' he agreed, smiling at her lazily. 'I'm home for good.'

'We've been hearing about your plans for redeveloping Sinclairs,' said Larry. 'Sounds quite a big job.'

Grey eyes rested for a moment on the hand lightly claiming Kerry's shoulder. 'It's going to take time,' he said. 'These things usually do. We're going to be pretty busy for the next few months.' He stifled a yawn with the back of his hand and made a rueful grimace. 'Sorry about that, but I've been travelling for twelve hours, almost non-stop. You won't mind if I leave you all to it and go to bed, I hope.'

'It's time we were all going home, anyway,' said Larry, taking his cue.

It took twenty minutes to get everyone organised into leaving, the girl who had been sitting beside Ross with the utmost reluctance.

'Didn't know you had such a dishy brother,' she murmured to Kerry at the door. 'Can't you get him to join the Group?'

'I doubt it,' Kerry answered, not bothering to correct her. 'His interests run along different lines.'

'You'll have to tell me what they are some time,' smiled the other. ''Night, Kerry. Thanks for the party.'

Larry was the last to leave, lingering in the hallway as car engines revved up outside. 'We have a couple of weeks before we start deciding on our next production,' he said. 'I am going to see you before that, aren't I?'

'Of course.' Conscious of Ross waiting for her back in the drawing room, she wanted him both to go and to stay. 'Phone me, Larry.'

He looked a little put out, unaccustomed to being fended off that way. 'How about Tuesday night? We can run out to the Pied Piper and have dinner.'

'All right, lovely.' At that moment she would have agreed to almost anything. 'Tuesday.'

He kissed her swiftly before she could draw back, seemed about to comment on her lack of response, then obviously thought better of it. Shutting the door after him. Kerry leaned her back against it for a moment. The last hour had taken more out of her than three nights as Eliza Doolittle on stage. For Ross to walk in like that without warning had been a shock her system could scarcely sustain. She was unprepared, both mentally and emotionally, for confrontation.

She closed her eyes, seeing his face against her lids as she tried to think what she was going to say to him. When she opened them again there was little change because he was standing in the drawing room doorway watching her, mouth as tight and straight as a trap.

'What game do you think you're playing?' he demanded. 'You're not going anywhere with anybody—Tuesday or any other night!' He waited for her to speak, brows drawing together when she failed to make any attempt. 'Kerry, answer me!'

Her voice came out low but carrying, filled with all the stored emotion of the past two weeks. 'You really thought you'd got it made, didn't you, Ross? You thought you'd come back here and click your fingers and I'd come running, ready to go along with anything you wanted!'

His jaw stiffened. 'What the hell are you talking about?'

'My Sinclair stock, that's what I'm talking about. You want control so badly you'd do anything to get it—including marrying me if absolutely essential.'

'In what way would that give me control?' His own voice was quiet too, dangerously so. 'The days are long gone when marriage automatically entitled a man to his wife's estate.'

'But besotted enough she could still bestow it. Isn't that what you said not so very long ago?'

'It's possible. I don't remember.' He studied her. 'You're trying to tell me you played up to me before I left just to see how far I'd go?'

'What do you think?'

'What I think,' he said, 'is you're lying through your teeth for some reason. And I'm going to find out why.'

He reached her before she could move, swinging her up off the floor and turning for the staircase. 'There's one place you won't lie to me for long.'

She resisted the urge to fight him by sheer effort of will, knowing he was too strong for her to break his grip so easily. Desperation clouded her mind as she looked at his face. If he once started making love to her she was capable of forgetting everything else. He knew that too. The only way of stopping him was to tell him what she knew. Even then she shrank from the thought. To see the guilt in his face, to know without a shadow of doubt that it *was* the truth—that would be the hardest part to bear.

Her bedroom was nearest the stairhead. He didn't bother switching on any lights, striding across to drop her on the bed with a force which drove the breath momentarily from her body. Pausing only to shrug off his jacket, he came down after her, hands ruthless as he pinned her under him.

His mouth on hers was impossible to resist, bringing response surging through her. Even as totally lacking in tenderness as this, she still wanted him, she acknowledged achingly. He overwhelmed her senses, melted every restraint, made her long for all he could give her. But that wasn't love. She couldn't love a man who had done what he had done.

'Is this how you made love to Margot?' she whispered

huskily as he lifted his lips from hers to move them over her thoat, and felt his whole body go rigid. It seemed an age before he spoke.

'How did you know about Margot?'

Up until that moment there must have been a small part of her which had clung to the hope that it wasn't true. With that gone the whole weight of hurt came down on her mind, blinding her to everything but the need to hurt back.

'She told me herself. The woman you were living with! She phoned me one night right out of the blue. She even knew why you were planning on marrying me. Sweet of you to tell her that much, just so she wouldn't feel too bad about things! After all, some things are so much more important than emotions, aren't they?'

He lifted his head then and looked at her, eyes cold and hard and totally without apology. 'The same night you phoned me, I assume? Why didn't you say all this then? I gather that was why you did phone?'

'Yes, it was. But when it came to it I couldn't.' Her voice shook. 'You don't even try to find an excuse, do you!'

'I don't have an excuse. I was living with her—or more to the point, she was living with me.'

'Oh God!' Kerry tried to move but found it impossible with his weight still pinning her. 'Get away from me, Ross,' she said through her teeth. 'Just get away!'

'I'll move when I'm ready to go,' he came back relentlessly, and hardened his grip on her, forcing her to lie still. 'All right, so maybe I should have told you. If I didn't it was because I knew you were unlikely to take it any way but how you are taking it.'

'What other way is there?' she demanded fiercely. 'What am I supposed to feel? You were planning on marrying *her* not so very long ago!'

'That's not true. If she told you that she was lying.'

She stared up at him for a long moment, trying to read

the mind behind the grey eyes, and not succeeding. 'She believed it,' she said at last. 'You must have given her cause to believe you were going to marry her. She said you were on vacation together when your father died. That was why you couldn't be reached at once.'

'That part's true enough, yes. I took her away for a few days to make things easier, that's all.'

'Make what easier?'

'Telling her it was over. It had been over for some time so far as I was concerned, but getting it through to her was something else again.' He sat up abruptly, pushing a hand through his hair in a gesture of resignation. 'What's the use? You wouldn't understand if I talked for a month.'

'You're right, I wouldn't.' Kerry came up on one elbow, limbs trembling. She felt numbed through, shorn of all emotion. 'You took her in because you wanted her and when *you'd* had enough you kicked her right out again! You're totally calculating, Ross. You know a lot about women—physically anyway—and you use that knowledge to suit your own ends. Well, here's one who won't play because she doesn't happen to think the game is worth the candle. And I don't care if that is a silly cliché, it's how I feel! You're not getting your hands on those shares any way!'

'Damn the shares.' His voice sounded harsh. He had his elbow resting on one knee, his head bent to the supporting hand half buried in his hair so that she couldn't see his face. 'I'd like to ram them down your throat!'

'Don't take your guilt out on me!' she shot back, and shrank against the pillow instinctively as he turned on her with rigidly compressed lips.

'Don't push it, Kerry. Self-righteousness doesn't help anything.'

'I'm not being self-righteous!'

'Yes, you are. And vindictive into the bargain, if I know

anything at all about women. You're going to fight me, aren't you?'

She gazed at him, hating him. 'That's all you really care about, isn't it? Margot, me—we're just nothing!'

Something flared for a second in the grey eyes and then died. 'If that's how you want to see it. But if you're not going to marry me, what I said before still goes. I'll break up any serious relationship you try to form with another man.'

'And what *I* said before still goes too,' she retorted fiercely. 'You can *try*! Now get out of here!'

He eyed her for one long calculated moment before reaching out and yanking her roughly towards him. Only when her struggles stopped and her body began signalling her helpless arousal did he finally lift his head to look at her with mockery in his eyes.

'That's one way I do have of getting to you, in spite of all your high ideals. I'd take you now if I didn't think leaving you high and dry will reckon more in the long run.'

She lay where he pushed her and watched him get up, wanting to say his name, to reach out her arms and have him come back to them, to forget everything else except right here and now. But the word wouldn't come, and it was too late anyway because he was going, closing the door hard behind him.

It was some time before she could bring herself to move. She felt bruised all over, physically and emotionally. Her dress was ripped along the seam. She took it off, letting it fall to the floor and kicking it out of the way. Damn Ross, she thought achingly. He shouldn't be able to make her feel this way. Not after what she knew about him. But he could and he did, and that was something else she was going to have to fight.

One thing was certain, no matter what she did about her Sinclair stock he had no intention of marrying this Margot either. He had used them both. With her it had been so shamefully quick too. He had sensed her attraction towards him and built on it swiftly and skilfully to a point where she had been unable to draw back, and all for one basic motive —to take control of Sinclairs into his own hands. It was an obsession with him, formed over the years of his self-exile, and almost realised. But not any more. She was going to fight him. Not just for Andrew's sake, but because he needed to realise he couldn't walk roughshod over other's emotions and get away with it.

It was a long night and not in any way a restful one. Kerry got up soon after seven, creeping out of the silent house to walk in the crisp, clear morning air for a couple of hours. Living in the same house as Ross was going to prove intolerable from now on, yet if she left it she forfeited her half of the estate. Or did they both forfeit? She tried to recall the precise wording of the will. Nine months of the year, Andrew had stipulated, but nothing beyond that. It was an odd condition anyhow. Why had he made it? The answer was only obvious if one accepted the fact that he had wanted to throw the two of them together as much as possible. Well, sorry, Andrew, but it wasn't going to work. It had been too much to expect. Her support he still had, but the name would remain the same.

Ross was cooking ham and eggs at the stove when she entered the house via the kitchen door. He gave her a brief, flicking glance which took in the shadows under her eyes, his mouth twisting a little.

'Want some of this?' he asked.

'If I do,' she said stiffly, 'I'll cook my own, thanks.'

'Stop being so bloody childish,' he came back equably. 'We have to live together and work together no matter how things are between us.'

'Only for nine months of the year,' she said, coming to a

sudden decision. 'The other three I imagine are optional. Under the circumstances, you'll understand if I take up my option right away and move out.'

The answer came cool and hard. 'You're not moving anywhere.'

'You can hardly stop me.'

'No?' He slid the ham on to the warmed plate, and broke an egg against the side of the pan with a deft flick of his wrist, opening the shell one-handed to let the contents slide into the hot fat. 'Time will tell.'

Kerry sought for some way to get at him, and found it, her tone matching his. 'If you're afraid of being lonely you could always send for Margot.'

The contraction of his jaw was a warning in itself. 'You don't know when to call stop, do you?'

'Do you?'

'Yes,' he said. 'I called it last night. So far at least.'

'And the rest?'

'I meant it. Every word. Try moving out of here and I'll fetch you back in a way that won't leave much doubt in anybody's mind of our relationship. Start seeing too much of that producer friend of yours and the same applies.'

'Larry would believe me rather than you.'

'Maybe you're right. There's one way of finding out.'

She looked at him helplessly, knowing herself inadequate. 'Ross, what's the use?'

'Call it persuasion,' he said. 'You can have as much freedom as you want if you'll make over that thirty per cent.' He brought the plate to the table and sat down, glancing at her with lifted brows as he picked up knife and fork. 'Why the big silence? You already knew that was all I was really after.'

Knowing it was one thing, having it underlined for her was another. 'Swine,' she said bitterly.

'Call me that again and I might start acting like one.' The

grey eyes moved over her with cool deliberation. 'Any time you need a reminder.'

There was no answer she could make. None, at least, that would help. Willpower might keep her emotionally immune, but nothing could stop her physical reactions if he took hold of her again the way he had done last night. It was a weakness he was not only aware of but more than willing to exploit if necessary.

She left him there in the kitchen and went up to her room, throwing herself on the bed to try and sort out something from the mess she was in. Gradually there grew in her the conviction that if there was going to be a fight at all it had to start right here and now. If she allowed him to intimidate her in any way she had as good as lost before they had even started.

They went through the rest of the morning in a state of armed neutrality. Kerry prepared lunch for two, but took her own on a tray upstairs and ate in solitude, unwilling to make the effort to face his mockery quite so soon. When she finally went down again he had shut himself in the study—or so she assumed from the faint sound of movement she could hear through the closed door.

Standing there she thought of all the things she could be doing herself, and rejected the lot because the house itself felt oppressive in a way it had never done before. On impulse, she donned outdoor things and left quietly, starting up the Allegro with a sense of reprieve if no very clear idea of where she was going.

At this time of the year the moors were in their glory, the purple heather stretching as far as the eye could see. Up there the nip of winter was already in the air, belying the clear blue skies and bright sunshine with its promise of hard times to come. Kerry left the car and climbed to a vantage point above the reservoir, finding a sheltered spot out of the wind to look out over the valley below.

From here one could only see a small section of the residential part of Medfield, the houses dwarfed by distance to doll size, with back gardens peopled by ants. Come tomorrow those people would all be back at their jobs, the staff of Sinclairs included. How would the latter react to the upheaval which was to be made of their working lives? Would they be glad or sorry to see change come to the Store? The younger ones perhaps—they were more likely to be adaptable to change—but what about the older generation? Some of them had been with Sinclairs the whole of their working lives.

It was the annual staff dinner-dance in a few weeks, she recalled. Andrew had always insisted on it being held in November before the Christmas rush got into final stride. Since her mother's death she had always attended it with him, sitting at the top table in company with the other members of top management and their wives, and afterwards dancing with the men in her party at a pace suited to their years rather than her own. One memorable year when she was twenty, a bold spirit from the sports department had been moved—or dared—to approach the table and ask her for a dance, only to be courteously but firmly turned down on her behalf by Andrew. A snob of the first order, had been her stepfather, she acknowledged now with rueful affection. It was difficult to imagine his son acting in quite the same autocratic manner.

Ross. The thought brought a swift concern. Would she be expected to attend the function with him as a partner? If so she absolutely refused to go! Common sense brought her down to earth again with a faint sigh. That was no answer. Of course she had to go, even if it did mean burying the hatchet with Ross for an evening. It would be expected of them.

She was cold in the strengthening wind by the time she got back down to the car, and eager for the warm protection of closed doors. The discovery that the keys were no longer in her pocket brought a swift dismay in no way tempered by the realisation that the most likely place for them to have fallen out was when she had been sitting up on the ridge.

The thought of making the steep and lengthy climb all over again made her heart sink, but there was nothing else for it short of walking five miles into town. She pulled her jacket closer about her and set off, keeping her eyes on the ground just in case the keys had fallen out on the way down.

The climb which before had taken her twenty minutes this time took over half an hour, and with no sign of the keys on the way. The shadows were lengthening across the valley by the time she reached her former seat, the air cold enough to make her wish she had brought gloves. Her dismay grew as her search of the immediate area revealed no keys. What on earth had happened to them? And what was she going to do if she couldn't find them at all?

The sun had set before she finally gave up. Wearily, she trekked back to the car, able to make out the time by the luminous dial of the dashboard clock as six twenty-five. By now Ross must have realised that she wasn't coming home for dinner. He would probably think she had done it on purpose, though why she should care *what* he thought she had no idea. Lights were winking in the valley, looking invitingly close. It was going to take her at least a couple of hours to get down there in the dark, she acknowledged fatalistically, then stiffened as the sound of a car engine coming around the bend behind her impinged on her consciousness.

It turned out to be a battered Ford with a young and equally unkempt-looking man driving it. Kerry was so glad to see anyone that all warning about strange men on dark and lonely roads vanished from her mind as she stepped forward waving her arms for him to stop.

'Hi,' he said cheerfully, winding down his window. 'Having trouble?'

'I've lost my keys,' she explained, warming to his apparent friendly concern. 'Can you give me a lift down to civilisation?'

'I can probably do better than that,' he said. 'Cars are my thing.' He switched off his engine and got out, tall and gangly in the ragged jeans and windcheater, long hair blowing back from a face Kerry instinctively trusted despite the frankly appreciative glance hc ran over her. 'Have to break a window to get you inside, natch!'

'Of course.' Kerry controlled a shiver as the wind cut through her. 'I'd have done that myself, but I'd have been no better off.'

He punched a hole in the far side passenger window and reached in to open the door, leaning across both seats to do the same with the driver's door. Kerry slid thankfully into the seat, glad to be out of the biting wind, and lifted the bonnet catch at her rescuer's command.

What he did down there in the engine she had no way of knowing, but within a moment or two there was a sudden splutter followed by a steadying throb, like music to Kerry's ears.

'Should be okay now,' he said, closing down the bonnet. 'Providing you don't stall it.'

'I won't,' she promised. She looked up at him through her wound-down window as he came alongside, smiling her gratitude. 'Thanks a million!'

'No sweat.' His eyes twinkled at her from beneath the tossed hair. 'You want to watch yourself out here on your own after dark, though. I could have been anybody.'

She had to laugh. 'Who are you anyway?'

'Name's Graham Bingham. I'm at Sheffield University, studying law.'

'You're quite a long way from base.'

'Been visiting some relatives. They've got a farm back up there.' He took his elbow off the roof and nodded to her. 'Watch how you go. I'll be behind you as far as the main road.'

Kerry watched him stride back to his own vehicle before setting her own into motion. That had been a really lucky break. Without his help she would have been committed to walking the five miles instead of riding in comfort.

He left her at the main road, turning left to her right and sticking out a hand in farewell. The town grew about her, residential areas gradually giving way to a closer build-up as she approached the centre, the street lights shimmering in a manner which denoted a possible frost later on. Perhaps fortunately there wasn't a lot of other traffic about when her engine suddenly coughed and died, leaving her to coast in as far towards the roadside as she could get before the wheels stopped turning.

With no way of turning on the ignition she couldn't be certain, but memory supplied enough of a reason for the abrupt cut-out. Petrol had been running low when she set off. She had intended to fill up at the first open garage, but not seeing one on the way out had decided to leave it until her return when a small detour would have brought her within reach of an all-night one. Too late now to think about that, of course. She was well and truly stuck. The clock said it was already well after seven, and taxis in Medfield tended to be almost non-existent outside the town centre at even the best of times.

She could always ring for one, of course, she reasoned, with her eyes on the telephone box a few yards further down the road. Yet what would that achieve? The car would still be stuck here, and it wasn't exactly in a good position to leave on a main road. That left her with one alternative—she could phone Ross and ask him to bring her the spare car keys. Had that been all it mightn't have been so bad, but when he did get here she was going to have to ask him to fetch petrol for her into the bargain. She could imagine his reaction to that.

She sat for several minutes more trying to think of some other way, but none occurred. Whichever way she went about things Ross was going to get to know about it some time. Eventually she forced herself into moving. If she lingered much longer there was always the chance that he would take it into his head to go out himself.

Typically, someone reached the phone box just ahead of her, and she spent a miserable and chilly ten minutes hanging around outside, not daring to go back and sit in the car in case another user came along. When she did finally get into the box it was to find she had neither two-pence pieces nor tens in her purse, which meant dialling the operator and reversing the charges.

Ross sounded unperturbed on being asked if he would accept the charges by the operator, but there was a distinct change of tone when he realised who was making the call.

'Where the devil are you?' he demanded.

Kerry explained the situation swiftly, and she hoped, succinctly, steeling herself for his sarcastic comment. All he said, however, was to wait where she was until he got there in about fifteen minutes—though where else he anticipated she might go she couldn't have said. She went back to the car and got in, all too aware that she was parked on a double yellow line and wondering if traffic wardens worked on Sunday evenings. Not that she could do much about it if one did come along. The car was going nowhere without petrol in its tank. And that fact she still had to impart to Ross.

He arrived in the Jaguar as a passing group of teenage louts were beginning to take an unhealthy interest in the Allegro and its sole occupant, banging on the window and jeering at her through the windscreen with lots of raucous laughter and ribald suggestions. The sight of him getting out of the car on the opposite side of the road gave them pause for consideration, but they didn't attempt to move on until he came purposefully across.

Kerry was trembling when she opened the door to him, as much from anger as anything else. 'The idiots!' she exclaimed. 'They think they're so clever!'

'That's just about it,' Ross agreed with what seemed to her then a galling lack of concern. 'They were trying to be big shots.' He leaned forward and put her spare key in the ignition, his face coming too close to hers for comfort. 'There you are. All set.'

'No, I'm not.' Her voice was small. 'I'm out of petrol—at least I think I am.'

He said something under his breath and turned the key to look at the gauge, straightening with a look of resignation. 'Where's the nearest garage likely to be open?'

'The Shell station,' she said. 'Out on the Ilkley Road. Do you know it?'

'I can find it.' He paused in the act of turning away, glancing back at her. 'Do you want to come with me?'

Kerry shook her head, gazing fixedly through the windscreen as she added stiffly, 'I'm sorry to put you to so much trouble.'

'Yeah.' The accent was deliberate. 'See you.'

Fuming, she watched the Jaguar move away up the road, saw it make the right turn through her driving mirror and vanish from view. It would take him perhaps ten minutes to fetch the petrol and get back. Right then she was more than tempted to leave the car standing and walk down to town for a bus up home.

The thought was parent to the deed. Without stopping to consider further, she got out of the car and locked the doors, slinging her bag over one shoulder with a defiance there was no one present to see. Let Ross figure out how to handle two vehicles. She was past caring.

It took longer than she had imagined to walk into the town centre where the bus terminal was situated, but only a couple of minutes to ascertain that the route she needed ran only every hour on Sunday evenings, with one only just gone. Returning to the car now was out of the question. Even if Ross was still there it was beyond her to do that amount of climbing down. Already she regretted the impulse which had brought her to this state. It had hardly been an adult way to act. That Ross would think the same was little comfort under the circumstances.

She was still standing there indecisively when the Jaguar pulled in at the head of the stand. The sound of the horn brought heads turning from all directions. Biting her lip, Kerry began to walk in the direction of the terminal exit, figuring Ross would have to back out and drive round in order to head her off. He didn't, of course; she should have known he wouldn't. She heard the engine rev and was bathed in the glare of his headlights as he came fast down the stand to draw up at her side and fling the nearside door open.

'Get in,' he said grimly.

Kerry got in, sinking into the soft leather and pulling the door closed in the same motion. She refused to look at him, too ashamed of her own behaviour to try brazening it out.

'I'm sorry,' she said. 'That was a stupid thing to do.'

The apology seemed to take the wind out of his sails for a moment. He looked at her sharply as if suspecting some kind of irony, then put the car into abrupt motion again. He didn't speak until they were back on the road and heading in the direction of the Allegro.

'Hungry?' he asked.

Expecting anything but that, she was too startled to be anything but honest. 'Yes, but . . .'

'There used to be a pub with a good restaurant attached

this side of town,' he went on. 'Still there?'

'Yes,' she said again. 'At least, if we're thinking of the same one.'

'About three miles out, if I remember. We'll collect your car on the way in again.' The curve of his lips held little humour. 'Save getting a meal when we get back to the house, and give us both chance to cool down. We need some time in neutral surroundings.'

The Allegro looked abandoned when they passed it. Kerry could imagine the impact that realisation had had on Ross on his return to the scene.

'How did you know where to look for me?' she asked diffidently, and received a brief glance.

'I didn't, I took a guess. Good thing there wasn't a bus standing in. I wasn't in any mood to care overmuch about your sensitivities.'

She was glad too. Being dragged off a bus in the middle of town would have proved distinctly embarrassing. Even now, it was quite possible that someone in the terminal to-night had recognised the two of them, and certainly those closer by could hardly have failed to realise something of the situation. Not that it mattered all that much; there were probably enough stories concerning their relationship circulating already throughout the Store.

'I'm not really dressed for dinner out,' she ventured after a while. 'I intended being back before six.'

'You'll do,' he said, this time without glancing her way. 'It isn't exactly a social occasion.'

They neither of them spoke again until they reached their destination. Kerry barely knew whether to be relieved or sorry to find the restaurant open for evening meals. She went to the cloakroom while Ross ordered drinks in the lounge bar. With fresh lipstick and a comb through her hair, she felt better though still a little frumpish in the slacks and white sweater she had on under her jacket, a feeling hardly improved upon by the sight of the elegant blonde talking with Ross at the bar when she got outside again. There was another man with her, but he appeared to have temporarily taken second place, standing by with an expression of ill-concealed disgruntlement on his face.

'There you are,' said Ross, catching sight of Kerry over the blonde's shoulder. 'I don't think you ever met Sharon West, did you?'

Kerry felt herself cringe inwardly from the cool blue gaze which swept over her as the other turned. The quilted peasant outfit with its full-sleeved blouse and toning boots made her slacks and sweater seem even more out of place. Sharon was tall for a woman, almost as tall as Ross himself when she stood up straight in the high-heeled boots, but her figure was faultless.

'So you're Ross's stepsister,' she said on a faintly disparaging note. 'No, we've never met before. I think you were still at school when I knew Ross.'

'That's right,' he agreed. 'Seven years ago. You weren't much older yourself, come to that. What happened to the London boutique, Sharon?'

'I decided there was less direct competition back here in Medfield,' she returned with a smile. 'I arrived about a couple of months after you left. Rather sudden, wasn't it?'

'You might say that.' He sounded unperturbed. 'Whereabouts are you?'

'West Street, where else?' The smile turned wry. 'I'm due for demolition under the new town centre planning scheme in a few weeks, so I'm looking for new premises right now.'

'Found anything suitable?'

'Not really. I could have the lease on one of the new shops going up in the same place, but that won't be for about six months and I can't afford to wait around that long.'

Kerry knew what was coming next before Ross spoke. It was there in his eyes. 'How would you feel about leasing floor space in the Store?' he asked. 'Could be good business for all of us.'

Sharon looked interested. 'I heard there were plans afoot to modernise Sinclairs. That's not a bad idea, Ross. What kind of footage did you have in mind?'

'We'll be moving Furs to a new location after the sale. That leaves a prime first floor position. I'm not sure of the exact footage, but we could work it out to joint satisfaction.'

'What sale?' Kerry asked, and wished she had kept her mouth shut as both heads turned towards her.

'We're overstocked in furs,' Ross said on a note of resigned tolerance which made her want to hit him. 'I told you that before I left for the States a couple of weeks ago. We cut our losses on the older stock by selling it off at bargain prices, and reduce the overall future holding. Considering the conservation campaigns in progress we're going to do better with simulations anyway.'

'Good thinking,' Sharon agreed. 'When can I come round and have a look at the space you're offering?'

'Make it tomorrow if you like. Say noon, then we can discuss details over lunch.'

'Fine, that's a date.' She turned back to her own companion with what seemed to Kerry an obvious reluctance. 'I suppose we'd better get on to this party. I only hope it isn't going to be as big a bore as the last one the Glovers gave.'

'Bill Glover?' Ross asked on a note of casual interest, and she looked back to him with new life in her.

'Of course, you knew Bill, didn't you? He married Jean Brompton three years ago.' She paused, eyes lighting up as the idea struck her. 'Why don't you come along to this party they're giving?'

His smile was dry. 'Without an invite?'

'I'm sure you'd have had one if Bill knew you were in

town. He's always the last to hear anything.' Her glance flickered in Kerry's direction. 'Both of you, of course.'

'Thank you.' Kerry kept a civil tone with an effort. 'I'm hardly prepared for a party.'

'Oh, nobody will mind. They're a very casual crowd. I didn't bother dressing up myself.'

Ross laughed. 'Just a rag you threw on? The same old Sharon!' The shake of his head held an air of regret. 'No gatecrashing tonight. We'll have a get-together at Underwood soon with all the old crowd. You can help fill in the names for me.'

'That sounds great! See you tomorrow, then.'

It didn't occur to Kerry until after they had gone that no one had seen fit to introduce her to Sharon's companion. Tensely she picked up the gin and orange Ross had ordered for her and tossed back half the contents at one swallow, feeling her throat contract as the spirit bit.

'You seem to be taking an awful lot for granted,' she said low-toned without lifting her eyes to look at him. 'Do you mind *not* announcing plans I know nothing about in front of other people?'

'Sorry about that,' he came back easily. 'It just came out in conversation.'

'Rather more than a conversation. You offered that woman a lease.'

'That woman,' he said on a slightly harder note, 'happens to be an old friend as well as a business proposition.'

'But you don't know anything about her business.'

'I'll naturally be doing some finding out before completing any deal.' He stirred impatiently. 'Save any arguments for later, will you, Kerry. I'm not in the mood right now.'

She wondered what he was in the mood for. Had seeing Sharon again brought good memories? The other woman was certainly very attractive, and obviously retained a favourable impression of former days. But Sharon didn't know what kind of man he had turned into since then. No one knew, except herself and Margot, and it was knowledge she could well have done without.

The meal was remarkably good, but Kerry did it scant justice. 'I've got past being hungry,' she said by way of excuse when Ross commented on her lack of appetite. 'I did a lot of walking this afternoon and I'm tired. Can we just go on back to the house?'

'Not yet.' He was leaning forward with his elbows on the table, hands cupping a brandy glass and an unreadable expression on his dark features. There was only one other couple in the intimately lit dining room, and they were all but hidden behind their own oak-backed settle. 'I said we needed neutral surroundings and you can't get much more neutral than this.' He paused, tone altering a fraction. 'We have to talk, Kerry.'

Her voice sounded brittle. 'About what?'

'You know damned well what!'

'If you mean the way you treated me last night, we'll take your apology as read if you like.' It took everything she had to achieve that cool note.

Ross turned his head and studied her face for a long hard moment. 'I'm not apologising for anything,' he said. 'You ask for everything you get.'

'Including being lied to?'

'I didn't lie to you.'

'Lying by omission is just as bad. There's no way you'd have told me about Margot if I hadn't found out.'

'So I wouldn't have told you. Confession isn't always a good thing. You'd have been happier not knowing.'

'Until you got careless, you mean? You're not trying to make out you'd have been content with one woman, are you?'

'I wouldn't have been getting a woman,' he said impatiently. 'I'd have been getting an idealistic little girl in need of a few short sharp lessons on life. Margot was over before I came back here and met you again. I can't alter what's past and gone.'

'You could have not started the thing with her in the first place—at least the living together part of it.'

His smile was faint. 'You wouldn't have minded my having taken her to bed providing she wasn't staying the night, is that it?'

'You know what I mean.'

'Sure, I know what you mean. Margot knew the score. It was a temporary arrangement until she found another apartment after her own got taken over. I made sure she had one to go to before I showed her the door.'

'You could have let her stay on in yours, seeing you were leaving it.'

'She couldn't have afforded it. Her job doesn't pay that kind of money.' There was cynicism in the line of his mouth. 'Part of the attraction, you might say.'

Kerry was silent for a moment, trying to sort out her emotions. Finally she said quietly, 'I don't really think it matters why, Ross. I'd never trust you.'

His shrug came carelessly. 'Maybe you're right. But I'm not going back on anything I said last night. Sinclairs stays with the family.'

'I don't think you'd keep that threat. What would old friends like Sharon think?'

'I don't really care what people like Sharon think. That makes the difference between us. You'd hate to hear the whispers behind your back—feel the sly glances.'

'Yes, I would,' she admitted, and hardened her tone with deliberation. 'But I'd even face up to that rather than give you what you want.'

'Only because you still don't believe I'd do it. Let's hope I don't have to convince you.' He stood up. 'I'll go and see about the bill. See you outside at the car.'

The Allegro was where they had left it. Ross poured in the contents of the can he had fetched from the garage and relocked the cap.

'You'd better go on round and fill up before going home,' he said. 'I'll follow you. Do you have enough cash on you?'

Kerry nodded, not trusting herself to speak. She got into the car and started the engine, realising the futility of telling Ross not to bother accompanying her. He would do as he thought fit. He was right, though, about her not believing him capable of what he had threatened. Not even Ross would go that far. What would it gain him?

CHAPTER SIX

IT was Ross's suggestion that they take both cars to th
Store next morning, leaving Kerry with the impression tha
he might have plans for the evening which did not includ
going home first.

'I've called a board meeting for eleven,' he said on arriva
'We're going to get this whole thing thrashed out from th
word go. If John and James come in on my side I'm goin
to go ahead regardless.'

'They won't,' Kerry returned with more assurance tha
she felt. 'And even if they do you can't just ignore my vote.

'I think we can. It would be sixty to forty. There's noth
ing in the rule book that stipulates an overall motion.'

'Nothing in *your* rule book, you mean.'

He put a finger on the door hold as the lift came to a hal
at the top floor, looking at her for a moment with an od
expression. 'Be rational about things.' he said at lengtl
'Regardless of how you feel about me personally, you wer
ready to go along with my plans for the Store a fortnigh
ago.'

'No,' she denied flatly. 'You assumed a little too muc
that afternoon in the boardroom. I read your report when
got home that evening, and I still didn't go along with a
of it. The changes you want to make are altogether to
radical.'

'You're talking purely from an emotional point of view.'

'One you'd know little about.'

'In this instance true enough. This place has to star
paying its way, Kerry.'

'It already does.'

'Only just. I could show a thirty per cent increase in ne

profit this next year given a free hand.'

'On paper.'

'And in practice.' Impatience shortened his tone. 'You're loing this to get at me and we both know it.'

'Don't flatter yourself,' she retorted. 'I'm doing it for 'our father—because it was what he intended I should do. won't go back on that trust, Ross. Not for you or for any- ne else.'

'He really left his mark on you, didn't he,' he said. 'I scaped, so he branded you in my place.' He paused, eyes hanging expression in a way which made her heart beat aster. 'Kerry, you don't owe him a thing. You gave him the vhole of this last six years since I left. Start living your wn life now—thinking your own thoughts. You know vhat I said in that report makes sense.'

Desperately Kerry shook her head. 'No!'

'So make things difficult.' He had lost patience altogether ow, his features grim. 'Just don't say I didn't warn you.'

He let the doors slide open, striding off along the corri- or without a backward glance, leaving Kerry to follow on ehind in her own time. She felt miserable but resolute. Nothing was going to change her mind. Nothing!

Surprisingly, it was John Barratt who saved the day for er later on. Normally he was content to allow his brother speak for both of them, when there was any speaking to e done at all, but today he obviously felt the need to state is own case.

'I've gone through your report very carefully,' he said to Ross, 'and while I can see the validity of all your argu- ents, I'm not sure the kind of store you plan is quite right r a town like Medfield. James doesn't fully agree with me, we came to an agreement between the two of us. If both ou and Kerry as equal stockholders want to go ahead, then e'll make it a unanimous vote.'

The snap of Ross's pencil breaking in two jerked Kerry's

pulses. He looked dryly at the pieces, then shrugged and dropped them into the blotter in front of him. 'Impasse,' he said. 'Kerry prefers to live in the past too.'

'It isn't a case of living in the past,' John protested. 'We've always done very well the way things are. Why put that at risk?'

'It won't stay that way for ever. People change. Needs change. The generation that keeps the place going at all is fast dying out, and the younger ones won't come without incentive.'

'Can't you give them that without undermining everything Sinclairs stands for?'

'Not if profits arc to rise accordingly. There aren't any half measures worth bothering with. The whole project has to be geared from the bottom up.'

'You never tried compromise before,' Kerry put in purposely. 'How can you be sure it wouldn't work?'

He gave her a stony glance. 'Because it's neither one thing nor the other. I think you've all probably got the wrong idea of what self-service means in this particular case. The assistance would be there if the customer needed it, but selection would be from open displays on her own initiative rather than over the counter, with payment at a central checkout.'

'I've shopped in stores like that,' Kerry said before anyone else could speak. 'Nine times out of ten it's almost impossible to find an assistant at all when you want one, and the pilfering must be astronomical!'

'Closed circuit TV would cut down on that.'

'And cost thousands.'

'We borrow what capital we need for overall expansion.'

'If we can get it.'

'We've already got it.' There was no particular inflection in the pronouncement. 'I went into that before I left. Bankers have foresight, thank God.'

Green eyes sparked. 'They're not on their own in looking ahead, are they? You really laid your plan of campaign well!'

'Not well enough, apparently. I forgot to take certain outside chances into account.'

James coughed, reminded them both that others were present. 'I'm not sure just what the trouble is between you two,' he said bluntly, 'but I'd rather it didn't get in the way of other matters. Andrew had no right to leave things in this state.'

'You mean in the hands of a woman, don't you?' Kerry put in with sarcasm. 'You three have a lot in common!'

James eyed her hardily before answering. 'You're not a woman yet, you're still a chit of a girl—and an insolent one into the bargain. Ross should put you across his knee!'

Kerry flushed, conscious of the mocking gaze on her from the head of the table. 'I've considered it,' Ross said, 'but I don't think that's the answer.'

'Then what is, man? We can't sit around here arguing the toss for ever!'

There was a pause, then Ross shrugged. 'Seems I'm going to have to settle for that compromise for the present. No self-service. Do I take it I have a free hand with regard to the rest?'

'So far as the two of us are concerned, I'd say yes.'

Meeting John's eyes, Kerry bit her lip. 'I'm sorry for blowing up like that,' she proffered, and received another sour look from James.

'Found your manners again, have you? It doesn't alter what I said. Andrew should never have done it.'

'Let's leave my father out of it, shall we?' Ross spoke quietly but with a finality that no one could fail to recognise. 'Kerry, are you going to go along?'

Her chin lifted. 'Providing you stick to your word.'

'No doubt you'll be around to see that I do.' He looked

at the time and pushed back his chair. 'That has to be it for now. I have an appointment in ten minutes.'

'And one after it,' Kerry observed with deliberation. 'I thought you never mixed business with pleasure.'

'Quite right, I don't.' He sounded unmoved. 'This is pure business, the pleasure could be in following James's advice. I'm going to Leeds later on this afternoon to see some people. I may stay overnight and come straight here in the morning.' To the cousins he added, 'I don't think there's much point in meeting again for at least a couple of months, unless something crops up that needs a board decision. By then I hope to be able to show some progress.'

Kerry refused to look in James' direction on leaving the room, too well aware of his smug satisfaction. When would she learn to stop fencing with Ross? He could flatten her so easily. She wondered if it were business or pleasure taking him to Leeds. Looking up old friends perhaps. A pity he couldn't stay there.

Wryly, she acknowledged how little she really meant that. Having Ross around was bad, but being without him at all was worse. If she married him she would at least have the compensation of some claim on his time in exchange for the loss of her own family name. Or would she? She could stir him physically now, but once sated that appetite might sicken and die, just the way it had with Margot.

She had forgotten her date with Larry until he rang on the Tuesday afternoon to remind her. It was on the tip of her tongue to make some excuse, but she hardened her will against the impulse. If she once began believing in Ross's threats she would be condemning herself to an unbearable situation. She liked Larry, and she needed the break.

'I'll pick you up at seven-thirty,' he said. 'The table is reserved for eight-thirty so we'll have time for a drink first.' He paused, voice taking on a softer note. 'I'm looking forward to seeing you, Kerry.'

'And me you,' she said, and meant it. With Larry she could relax and forget for a while. She looked up sharply as Ross came through from his own office, met the grey eyes and felt herself stiffen. 'Seven-thirty,' she repeated with emphasis. ' 'Bye, Larry.'

Ross had crossed to drop a letter on Kate Anthony's desk. 'Going somewhere?' he asked.

'Yes. Out to dinner. I'm afraid you'll either have to get your own or eat out yourself.'

'I'll see how I feel.'

She looked at him with a faint sense of anti-climax. 'No warnings?' she asked with irony. 'No threats of what you might tell him about us?'

His shrug was almost goodhumoured. 'One swallow doesn't make a summer. If I thought you were in any danger of falling for the guy it might be different.'

'What makes you so sure I'm not?'

He studied her coolly, leaning against the front edge of the desk with both hands supporting his weight. 'The fact that you're already in love with another man.'

Warmth travelled fast under her skin. 'Modesty isn't your strong point, is it?' she said scathingly, and saw his smile come slow and mocking.

'I didn't mention my name.'

'It's what you were implying.'

'And you'd deny it, of course. You'd rather persuade yourself you hate my guts because I turn out to have a past you don't care for. Has it ever occurred to you that I might not have been able to rouse you the way I obviously can without a little former experience?'

Kerry was silent for a long moment, barely trusting herself to speak. 'You don't know what love really is, do you?' she said at last on a low, unsteady note. 'You think it's purely physical.'

'Mostly physical,' he corrected. 'You wouldn't want me

if I couldn't make love to you, so don't try pretending my mind is more important to you.'

'Your attitudes are. I can't say emotions, because you don't have any!'

'You're wrong, you know. I've an absolute yearning to bring you down to earth with a bang. One of these days I'm going to do it too, regardless.'

'Of what?'

'Of what else gets in the way.' There was a brief pause before he straightened, his mood deliberately lightening. 'So remember, the next time I click my fingers I want you to come running. It will save a lot of time in the long run.'

'Go to hell,' she said thickly.

He laughed. 'If I do I'll take you with me. Behave yourself tonight and I might let you go on seeing your Larry.'

Kate Anthony's return to the office at that point saved her from the effort of finding a rejoinder. Ross nodded pleasantly to the newcomer and left, but there was no dispelling the atmosphere he had created as easily. Kerry knew Kate sensed something in the air, but the older woman was far too discreet to ask any questions. She wished suddenly that she could confide in her, ask her advice. Yet what advice could anyone give her?

Ross still hadn't come home by the time Larry arrived to pick her up as promised. She tried to tell herself she didn't care where he had gone, and knew she lied. Despite his denials, she had a strong suspicion that Sharon West attracted him more than a little. Old flames had a way of flaring up again when stirred.

She made an effort to throw off despondency by concentrating on her own companion for the evening, an interest which Larry accepted wholly at face value.

'It's strange,' he said at one point, 'how different people turn out to be when you get to know them. Up until a few weeks ago you always seemed so aloof—as if letting you hair down and having some fun was completely beyond you.'

Kerry laughed. 'I'm not exactly a swinger now.'

'No, but you're good company.' His tone took on an underlying seriousness. 'We have a lot in common, the two of us, wouldn't you say?'

'Well, yes, I suppose we do.' She was wary, not quite certain what might be coming next. 'We're both interested in drama, for one thing.'

'Oh, I meant in more ways than that. We like the same kind of things, like this place for instance. It isn't everyone's cup of tea because there's no entertainment.'

'You mean it wasn't Heather's?' she asked softly, and he shrugged.

'Heather preferred going to discos to eating out. She doesn't have a lot of small talk.'

'But fun to be with?'

'Yes.' It was obvious that he didn't want to talk about past girl-friends. 'How are plans coming along for Sinclairs?'

Something cooled inside her. 'You'd have to talk to Ross about that. He has things in hand.'

'But you know what he's doing, surely?'

'I know what he isn't doing.' It was out before she thought about it. She saw his eyebrows lift a fraction, and felt impelled to explain. 'He wants to make the Store over into a counterpart of the one he ran in the States—strip it of all individuality.'

'In the interests of higher profits, I assume?'

'That's what he says.'

'With his experience of the retail business he should know what he's talking about.'

Her mouth tightened a little. 'I should have known you'd be on his side!'

'It isn't a case of taking sides. Every business has to move with the times if it's to stay viable. Sinclairs' overheads must be astronomical in comparison with profits. Modernisation redresses the balance.'

'It isn't what Andrew would have wanted.'

'Your stepfather isn't here any more,' Larry pointed out. 'You can't live his life over again for him, Kerry.'

'In other words, you think I should give Ross his head and let him do exactly as he likes.'

He hesitated, eyeing her in some uncertainty. 'Up to a point,' he compromised at length. 'See how things go before you make any final decisions.' His smile was deliberately light. 'Anyway, let's forget business for tonight. I thought we might try something more up to date for the next production, so I'm asking everybody to come to the next meeting armed with a couple of suggestions.'

Still a little tense, Kerry allowed herself to be drawn into a discussion on the merits of Larry's own particular choices which took them safely through the next half hour.

They were back at Underwood before eleven-thirty. Faced with the light in the hall, Kerry knew a sudden reluctance to be alone with Ross right away. It was a cool night and the car heater had been playing up all the way back. Larry was not loath to agree to her suggestion of coffee before he made his way home.

Ross was through in the sitting room, which he seemed to prefer. He greeted the two of them without surprise.

'Haven't been in long myself,' he said without offering any further information. 'Quite nippy out, isn't it?'

Kerry left the two of them chatting while she went through to the kitchen to make the coffee. By the time she got back they were discussing Hall's Engineering with every sign of real interest on Ross's part.

'So you're the obvious choice to take over the managing directorship when your uncle retires,' he said as he moved forward to take the tray from her and deposit it on a table.

'ust for a second grey eyes met green, the former veiled. How old is he?'

'Sixty-four,' Larry admitted, and gave vent to a faintly vry smile. 'Not that I can see him doing it. He's the kind o go on till he drops.' He realised suddenly what he had aid and looked a little uncomfortable. 'Sorry, I was for- ;etting you'd just lost your father that way.'

'That's okay.' Ross's expression hadn't altered. 'You ould hold him up as an example to your uncle. If he'd etired at sixty-five he might still have been here.'

He might have done, Kerry wanted to say, had his son ɪeen prepared to give and take a little more. She contented ɪerself instead with a dry smile as she handed him his cof- ee, knowing it had struck home by the fleeting glint in his yes. She took her own cup to a seat at Larry's side on the ofa, assuming a casual air. Those threats Ross had made ɪeant nothing. She had never really imagined they did. He ad welcomed Larry into the house as if nothing at all were miss with the situation, had even gone out of his way ɔ make him feel at home. No, she had called his bluff and ɪat was that. She wondered why the knowledge brought o satisfaction.

'Saturday?' Larry asked when she saw him to the door n leaving. 'We can go into Leeds.' He took her agreement ɔr granted, pulling her towards him to kiss her long and ngeringly, barely seeming to notice her half-hearted re- ɔonse. 'From now on,' he said when he eventually lifted is head from hers, 'I intend to monopolise your time, :erry Rendal.'

Ross was standing where they had left him in front of the re when she got back to the sitting room. She didn't look : him as she began stacking the tray.

'You look well kissed,' he observed. 'Enjoy it?'

'Yes,' she said, and then on a stronger note, 'Yes, I did.

Larry doesn't force his attentions where they might not be welcome.'

'Neither do I.' His tone was quiet. 'But I've no intention of providing you with an example tonight, so you can rest easy.'

'Scared you might not match up?' she flashed.

'You won't goad me into it either,' he said, still without change of expression. 'Any more than you managed to goad me into putting your boy-friend in the picture by bringing him back here. He might be showing all the signs of getting in deep, but I doubt if you are.'

'Because I'm already in love with you?'

'You can call it what you like. I only know I could take you up to bed right now and have you willing within minutes, which I'd say is more than friend Larry could get out of you.'

Kerry choked back the swift surge of longing. 'Physically perhaps. After all, you've had plenty of practice. But it still wouldn't get you what you want.'

'I know. That's why I'm not going to bother. What was it you said about the game being worth the candle?'

She gazed at him; hating him, loving him, wanting him, all at the same time. At last she said huskily, 'If Larry ever asks me I'm going to marry him, and nothing you can say or do will stop me.'

He shrugged. 'We'll see, shall we? Right now I'm going to bed. I'll take that through on the way.'

Kerry swung the tray up and away from his outstretched hand. 'I'll take it through myself, thanks.'

'All right then, take it. I'm not going to argue with you over a tray.' He sounded indifferent. 'Goodnight.'

She didn't answer. Right then she felt too thoroughly miserable to use the word good about anything.

Snow came early on higher ground that year. By the second week in November there had already been two moderate falls to coat the surrounding hills, although the town itself had escaped all but a light sprinkling.

Because of the pre-Christmas rush, many of the changes scheduled for Sinclairs had to be put off until the New Year, but others went on apace. The fur sale was aided not a little by the inclement weather, clearing the department of most of its older stock and creating a great deal of interest in a new range of simulations. Afterwards, the whole department was moved lock, stock and barrel to another position and the former site revamped for the West Boutique to move in.

Reluctant though she was to find anything in the idea of leased shops, Kerry had to admit that never before had Sinclairs seen as much of the younger generation as it began to do now. The new snack bar-coffee shop did an excellent service from the word go, bringing a smile even to the dour features of the chief accountant when relating the first month's profits. So far the changes had been gradual enough to be relatively unobtrusive, but Kerry was well aware that all that would change once the New Year period was over. The January sales would clear out much dead stock and leave room for the more profitable lines. In the meantime, the whole stock control system was receiving a thorough investigation in readiness for the time when it too would be called upon to incorporate modified ideas.

Contrary to Kerry's expectations, the majority of the staff seemed to find the whole thing exhilarating. Only the older end showed any tendency to cling to established customs and methods, horrified and dismayed by what those at the 'top' were doing to their beloved store. Kerry knew she was blamed equally along with Ross and could do nothing to correct the impression. But at least they would not have to suffer the indignity of seeing self-service installed, she comforted herself. In that, if in nothing else, she had the last word.

Living with Ross these last few weeks had not been too difficult because she saw relatively little of him. He was out most evenings, and those he spent in were generally in the seclusion of the study. She told herself she didn't care and knew she lied. Something vital had gone out of her life when Ross had lost interest in pursuing her. Once or twice he came close to wishing she had ignored the malicious phone call and gone ahead and married him anyway, yet she knew deep down that it would not have taken long for such a marriage to founder.

Had she cared to try she was fairly confident that she could make Ross want her again, but that was no answer to what really ailed her. Larry was a consolation of sorts because it was increasingly obvious that he really did care. It was there in the way he held himself in check when he kissed her, once going so far as to chide her for responding too warmly.

'It's difficult enough,' he said regretfully, 'without being tempted this way. You're a lovely, sensual girl, Kerry, and there's nothing I'd like better than to make complete love to you, but you're not the kind of girl one has that kind of relationship with.'

Sensual, Kerry thought later, remembering. She hadn't been before Ross came home—not at least that she knew. That hadn't been Larry she'd been kissing tonight, it had been Ross. Right now, lying here in bed, her whole body ached for him. He was just along the landing; all she had to do was to go to him. Yet she knew she wouldn't. As Larry had said, she wasn't cut out for that kind of relationship.

The annual staff dinner dance was generally held in the restaurant at the end of November. That being impractical this year, Ross hired the banqueting room at the town hall for the occasion, together with one of the ante-rooms to be put to use as a disco for the younger element. A committee elected from among the staff themselves took care of all other arrangements, from choosing the menu right down to hiring two different sets of musicians for the evening. An idea with method behind it, as Ross freely admitted. If anything went wrong the committee would be blamed rather than management.

'It must be costing twice as much as other years,' Kerry remarked a little slyly one afternoon when Arthur Fielding was in the Chairman's office, and saw from the older man's compressed lips that he agreed.

Ross was unmoved. 'It's a once-a-year event and we're going to be calling on them all for a great deal of concerted effort during the next few months.'

'Reward in advance?' she queried. 'Do you think that works?'

'The word you're looking for is bribe,' he came back equably. 'And I hardly regard a gala evening as that. Do what the rest will do, relax and enjoy it.'

She said it without stopping to consider, 'I'm not sure I shall be going.'

He looked at her hardily for a moment before replying. 'You'll be going. We'll all be going. That's right, isn't it, Arthur?'

'Er—yes,' agreed the accountant, who obviously was not over-keen on the idea. 'If you think it necessary.'

'I do.' Ross's tone brooked no discussion on the matter. 'Incidentally, the committee decided individual round tables to seat twelve were a better idea than the usual spurs. You and your wife will be on the top table, of course, so it won't affect you, but it should work out pretty well, I think. Might take the catering staff a few minutes longer to clear the room ready for dancing afterwards, but there'll be the disco and bar to visit while people are waiting.'

Kerry controlled a grin as the accountant passed her on his way out. Trying to imagine Arthur Fielding and his equally dour wife moving to the rhythm of beat music in a discotheque took some doing. When she looked up again Ross was watching her with an odd expression.

'First time you've smiled in this office for at least a fortnight,' he observed.

'Perhaps the first time I've considered there was anything much to smile about,' she came back, recovering fast. 'You don't need me any more, do you?' She was already moving to the door as she spoke.

'Just to complete your day, you'll be sitting alongside me at the top table on Saturday,' he said dryly. 'So if you want to invite Larry he's going to have to sit with someone else.'

Kerry caught herself up from what she had been about to say, aware that he was waiting for her to argue about it. 'I doubt very much if Larry would want to come anyway. He considers their own staff affairs boring enough.'

'If they are he should maybe do something about livening them up.'

She flared at once. 'Just because you didn't like him very much ...'

'I never said I didn't like him. As a matter of fact, he's not at all a bad guy. Under other circumstances ...' He left it there, adding obliquely, 'You're seeing a lot of him these days, aren't you.' It was a statement, not a question.

Her chin lifted. 'So what if I am?'

His smile was disarming. 'Just an observation. I'd say it was about time we gave that party I talked about once. Between us we should come up with a sizeable guest list. Let's make it the first weekend in December as a build-up to Christmas festivities. Enough time for you to contact all those you'd want to come?'

'Considering I see most of them every week, more than enough.' She studied him, a little nonplussed. 'Do you really think the atmosphere at Underwood lends itself to a party?'

'What atmosphere?'

'You know what I mean.'

'No,' he said, 'I don't think I do. That's a date, then. And don't worry about catering. I'll get a local firm in.'

Back in her own office, Kerry found herself wondering just who Ross would be inviting to this party. Sharon West would be one for certain. The two of them appeared to have been very discreet these last weeks, but she was convinced that Sharon was the cause of his spending so much time away from the house in the evening. She knew the other had her own flat the west side of Medfield, and had been tempted once or twice to ask him why he didn't reverse his previous arrangement and move in with her for six months.

Seen in retrospect, the sheer malice behind that phone call from Detroit was as plain as day. Margot must have known she had no chance of regaining Ross's interest but had seen no reason to let her successor entertain any illusions. Kerry doubted if he would have told Sharon about that six months with another woman—although perhaps *she* wouldn't mind anyway.

And that wasn't exactly a charitable attitude on her part, she acknowledged wearily. She didn't know Sharon well enough to pass any kind of judgment on her.

It was drama rehearsal again that night. This time they had chosen a light comedy in a modern setting, which still had to be cast. Larry had wanted her to play the lead again, but she had already refused point blank. Let someone else have the honour.

Kerry mentioned the coming party before the group dispersed for the night, and was gratified by the eager acceptance.

'I wondered when I was going to get to meet that brother of yours again,' said Jill Willet, the girl who had shown so much interest the last time. 'He doesn't spread himself around very far, does he?'

'No,' Kerry returned with unwonted shortness. 'And he's only my stepbrother.'

'Same thing just about.' Speculation lit the other girl's eyes for a moment. 'Unless you fancy him yourself?'

It was Larry who answered for her. 'Don't be so damned ridiculous! She was just putting the record straight, that's all.'

'Well, that's all right, then.' Jill was quite unabashed. 'Leaves me a clear field.'

Kerry could have disillusioned her on that score but didn't bother. Jill would discover for herself soon enough that where Ross was concerned there was no such thing as a clear field. He simply kept his options open.

Heather Wyatt was the only one to refuse the invitation, hardly bothering to conceal her antipathy towards Kerry. 'Afraid I'm already booked that night,' she said airily. 'Still, I'm sure I'll hardly be missed.' Her glance went from her to Larry and back again, her smile never faltering. 'When are you two going to give us something to celebrate?'

'Sooner than you might think,' Larry said before Kerry could open her mouth. He took her arm possessively. 'Time we were all going. The verger wants to lock up.'

Once again he had invited a few members back to his flat for a drink. It was some time before Kerry could get a word with him alone.

'You shouldn't have said what you did to Heather,' she protested. 'She's likely to make something of it.'

'What if she does?' He was smiling but the blue eyes were serious. 'Kerry, my uncle wants to meet you. Will you come out to dinner at the house this coming Friday?'

She attempted a light note, aware of conflicting emotions. 'Am I to be vetted?'

He laughed. 'I suppose you could call it that. He doesn't

trust my judgment where women are concerned, although your being Andrew Sinclair's stepdaughter gives you a head start.'

'I could still be anyone.'

If Larry registered the faint acidity in her tone he didn't show it. 'He'll love you. He can't fail to.'

And what if he didn't? Kerry wondered. Would that affect Larry's regard?

'I'll pick you up at seven,' he said, taking her agreement for granted. 'And don't worry, his bark is far worse than his bite.'

Later, seeing her down to the car, he repeated the arrangement, adding this time, 'It won't be just the two of us. Alderman Perry and his wife will be there, plus several others.'

'And all around your uncle's generation?' she asked.

'Well, yes, I suppose they are.' He looked at her uncertainly. 'Does it really matter for one evening?'

'No, of course not.' She smiled at him warmly, pushing her own feelings to the back of her mind. 'I won't let you down, Larry.'

'I know that.' He kissed her, letting her go with reluctance. ' 'Night, darling.'

Kerry drove home in a troubled frame of mind. That this summons on Friday held significance she didn't doubt for a moment. Larry must have intimated to his uncle that he was serious enough about her to necessitate closer investigation. She supposed old Mr Hall couldn't be blamed too much for wanting to see for himself what kind of girl his nephew was contemplating tying himself up with. The real problem was in trying to decide just how she herself felt about that possibility. She liked Larry a lot, and that was surely a better basis for marriage than the kind of hold Ross had over her. Love could grow from liking, but never the other way round.

CHAPTER SEVEN

THE Jaguar was already in the garage when she got home. She parked the Allegro neatly alongside and closed the doors again, then stood for a moment swinging her keys and looking at the house. From the lack of lights in the front, he was either through in the sitting room or upstairs in his own room. Neither way would she have to see him or talk to him, yet still she hesitated. Underwood was something else she had to think about if she married Larry. She doubted if he would be content to reside here, large enough though the place was. On the other hand, he hadn't even asked her yet, and might not at all if his uncle didn't give him the green light on Friday. No use crossing bridges before one came to them.

Ross's bedroom door was closed when she went upstairs, but a light showed beneath it. She went into her own room and put a further barrier between them, wishing she could block off her emotions in the same way.

She lingered longer than usual in the bath, soaking away mental as well as physical fatigue, feeling the lethargy creeping into her limbs. Too tired for more than a perfunctory rub when she finally got out, she knotted the towel about her to finish the job while she went through to the bedroom to find a fresh nightdress. The sight of Ross sitting on her bed with his back against the padded rest brought her up short in the doorway. H was wearing dark blue jugoda-style pyjamas, the jacket fallen open to the waist on a heavy triangle of hair, a pair of leather slippers on his leisurely crossed feet.

'I thought you were going to stay in there all night,' he

said. 'Five more minutes and I was going to come and get you out.'

Kerry found her voice, aware of the quick fire beat of her heart. 'The only getting out that's going to be done is you from here!'

'Not until we've cleared up a few outstanding matters.'

'Such as what?'

'You know what.' His glance moved over her, his lips pulling into a faint smile at the colour which swept her face. 'I want you, Kerry, and I'm sick of waiting. Take that off and come to bed. We can sort out the rest in the morning.'

She didn't move, clutching at the slipping towel in swiftly mounting anger. '*You* want? Is that all that concerns you?'

'No—though at the moment it's a prime consideration.'

'More so than Sinclairs?' she retorted with sarcasm, and saw the fleeting wrynesss touch his mouth.

'Priorities take on different aspects from different angles. That pride of yours won't be mollified by words, so I'm resorting to action. After I've made love to you, you might be in a better frame of mind to listen.'

'There's nothing you could say at any time that I'd want to hear!'

'That's a risk I'll have to take.' He paused, brow lifting. 'Are you coming to me or do I come to you?'

He meant it, Kerry realised. He really meant it! Life returned to her limbs in a burst of movement which took her back through the doorway and slammed the door in his face. Her fingers were trembling as she slid the bolt. If she had to stay in here all night she'd do just that. Anything rather than give him the opportunity to undermine her defences the way he so certainly could.

She didn't hear him moving until the door handle depressed. It stayed depressed as his shoulder met the wood with sufficient force to spring the bolt from its moorings.

'So I come to you,' he said on a rueful note as he rubbed the shoulder. 'It never looks so much of a stunt on film!'

'Ross, stop this.' Her voice held an element of pleading. 'It's gone beyond a joke!'

'It went beyond that a long time ago,' he came back. 'Dad wanted us to share everything, didn't he?'

'Not like this.'

'Well, you won't marry me, so this is all that's left.' He came over to where she stood against the far wall, a look in his eyes she recognised only too well. She let go of the towel to defend herself as he pulled her to him, and felt it slip down to her waist, held there only by the rough knot she had tied in it.

Then he was kissing her and everything else began slipping, including her will-power. The male scent of him was in her nostrils, tangy and emotive, the pressure of his hands warm against her bare back. The hair on his chest felt wiry to her breasts, tingling her skin as if charged with minute electric currents. Almost unconsciously she moved closer to him, wanting the contact all the way through her, but he held her away, smiling down into her half closed eyes. 'Slowly, honey, slowly.'

The struggle was still going on inside her, but somehow she couldn't bring her limbs to obey the urge to stop him from doing what he was doing. She gave a small moan when he lifted a hand to her breast, his touch almost a pain.

'They're perfect,' he said softly. 'Just right to hold.' He stroked a thumb very gently across her nipple, watching her face with the smile growing in his eyes. 'You're not going to fight me any more, are you, Kerry? You want this as much as I do. *Don't* you?'

'Yes.' It was little more that a whisper. Her whole being seemed centred immediately beneath that caressing hand.

She felt his other hand move to her waist and find the knot of the towel, and a small sound of protest broke from her lips. 'No, Ross ... please!'

'All right,' he said. 'I'll take it off in bed. I'll even turn the light out if it will make you feel better.'

'I'm sorry,' she murmured with constraint. 'I—I can't help it.'

'You'll learn. I'll teach you to be proud of your body, not self-conscious over showing it to me. You're beautiful, Kerry—a lovely, sensuous woman, with nothing ever to feel ashamed about. I want to know you, darling. And I want you to know me.' He kissed her again, lips tender. 'Let's go to bed.'

The strident ring of the telephone in the bedroom cut through the end of the last word, making them both start. For Kerry at least the shock was like a douse of cold water, stiffening her body in his arms.

'Who the hell?...' Ross exclaimed. 'For God's sake, it's one o'clock in the morning!' He let go of her with reluctance as the instrument went on ringing, striding through to lift the receiver and clip out the single word. 'Yes?'

Slowly Kerry pulled up the towel and tightened the knot to hold it secure. She could feel Ross watching her through the opened door but couldn't bring herself to lift her head and look back at him.

'I see,' she heard him say. 'Well, can't you handle it?' A pause while he listened and when he spoke again his tone was different—resigned. 'All right, I'll be there in about twenty minutes.' The bang of the receiver must have made the caller wince.

'There's been an attempted break-in at the Store,' he said. 'The police contacted Arnold Gregson, but they want me down there too.' He came back to the doorway, leaning a hand against the jamb as he studied her averted face. 'Look at me, Kerry,' he said. When she made no move to comply he came to her, taking her chin in his hand and lifting her head. The grey eyes held a mixture of expressions. 'I'm sorry about this. It's hardly the way I'd have planned things to happen.'

'You're going to be late,' she said, and thought how oddly matter-of-fact her voice sounded. 'Hadn't you better get dressed?'

The pause was strained. 'I suppose I had,' he said at last. 'Try not to be asleep when I get back, will you?'

Sleep? That was almost funny. Kerry doubted if she would sleep at all that night. 'I'll try,' she said.

'Good girl.' He gave a faint smile. 'I shouldn't be too long. Can't imagine why they'd need me there anyway. Gregson should have been able to deal with things.'

She was thankful that he hadn't. Without that phone call she would have been lost. Not that regrets would have emerged before morning, she acknowledged painfully. Ross had woven his spell only too well.

He didn't come back to her room before leaving the house, whether from sensitivity on her behalf or simple lack of time she had no way of being sure. Kerry waited until the car engine had died away into the distance before slowly relaxing the tension in her body. But not for long, she reminded herself. He would be back. And before that she had to find some way of keeping him away from her. She was under no illusion whatsoever over his powers of persuasion.

He was gone almost two hours. Lying in bed, she heard the car draw up round the front of the house, and the thud of a door closing. Then he was in the house and coming up the stairs, each footstep echoing the beat of her heart. Head half turned into the pillow, she feigned sleep as he came on into her room, praying that no involuntary flutter of an eyelid would give her away.

'Kerry?' he said softly without turning on the light. He

came closer when she failed to respond, putting a light hand on her shoulder, the smile there in his voice. 'Hey, sleepyhead, I broke all records getting back here!'

Kerry stirred a little and muttered something—she wasn't even sure what—before settling back into the same even rhythm of breathing. Even without being able to see him she could sense his disconcertion.

The bottle standing on her bedside table must have caught his eye then, for he took his hand away to pick something up, switching on the side lamp in order to read the label. The silence was so lengthy she was almost tempted to open her eyes to see if he was still there. When he did move it was abruptly, dropping the bottle back on to the table with a total disregard for the glass top and switching off the light again. Then he went, closing the door behind him and leaving her there in the darkness. She had never felt so alone as she did at that moment.

She slept a little before morning, waking to the sound of rain lashing against the windows. A shower refreshed her physically if not emotionally. She wondered how she would have been feeling this morning had that phone call not broken things up last night. Certainly no worse that she felt now. Perhaps by now matters would have been settled between them in more ways than just the one. Marriage with Ross might not be a bed of roses, but the pros could outweigh the cons on average.

She was first downstairs. Ross came into the kitchen as she was laying bacon on the grill, a faint compression still lingering around his mouth.

'I took the sleeping tablets from your room and got rid of them,' he said abruptly. 'I should have done it last night. Where did you get hold of them in the first place?'

'They were your father's,' she said, concentrating on the bacon. 'He didn't use them very often, only when he really needed to. They were in his bathroom cabinet still.'

'How many did you take?'

She hesitated, not at all sure what the correct dosage was and regretting that she hadn't checked on the bottle first. The apparent 'dead to the world' effect had to be accounted for. 'Two,' she hazarded.

'You little fool!' His tone was harsh. 'It says one only on the bottle!' He came over and took the bacon tongs out of her hand, turning her into the light to study her face, a cold anger in his eyes. 'Do you feel all right?'

'Yes.' She dared say no more than that.

'You were lucky.' The pause was brief, his expression unchanging. '*Why*, Kerry?'

'Because I knew you'd expect to take up where you left off, and I wasn't going to sit around waiting your pleasure.' Her voice quivered on the last; she had to force herself to hold his gaze. 'I'm not another Margot, Ross. I've no intention of being used whenever you happen to feel like it. We may be living in the same house, but from now on that's as far as it goes.'

He said cruelly, 'That's not what you wanted last night.'

The flush started deep, but she refused to let it confuse her. 'I'm quite sure you're capable of making any female lose sight of her better instincts in certain circumstances. It's nothing to be proud of. Perhaps you thought I might feel bound to take the Sinclair name after spending the night with you.'

Some fleeting expression crossed his features. 'Perhaps I hoped,' he said on a softer note.

'All right then, hoped.' She wasn't giving an inch. 'You'd do anything to keep that stock in the family, wouldn't you?'

'You really think that was the only reason?'

'What other?' She infused irony into her voice. 'You're certainly not in love with me.'

It was a moment before he answered, his fingers hard on her shoulders, the expression in his eyes hard to decipher.

'If I told you I was, would you believe me?'

'Not for a minute.'

'That's what I thought.' He released her, his shrug indifferent. 'So we're back to square one.'

'That's right.' She hardened herself to add, 'And in case you're planning any further campaign, I should warn you now that I'm going to marry Larry.'

Grey eyes narrowed. 'He's asked you?'

'Let's just say I know he's going to. And I'm going to say yes, and there's no way you're going to stop it, Ross.'

He didn't answer, just stood there looking at her for a long moment. When he did speak it was without inflection. 'Just in case you're wondering, they caught the men involved in last night's attempt. Lucky for Sinclairs they didn't succeed.'

'Damn Sinclairs,' she came back forcefully. 'It's all you care about!'

His shrug signified agreement. 'You'd better get that bacon under the grill,' he said, 'if we're going to eat at all this morning.'

They ate in silence, and left the house in silence, taking separate cars as a matter of course. Watching the Jaguar's tail end vanish ahead of her, Kerry wondered bleakly if marriage with Larry Hall could ever provide her with a fraction of the depth of feeling she had found in Ross's arms last night.

Dinner at The Larches turned out to be far less of an ordeal than Kerry had anticipated. Not being certain how far she would be expected to dress up to the occasion. she compromised with a black velvet skirt and matching top, filling in the modestly scooped neckline with a cameo pinned to a narrow black velvet ribbon. Mr Hall was faintly intimidating at first, until one realised that his Yorkshire bluntness concealed a basically tolerant disposition. That Larry held a position of some esteem in his uncle's regard was self-evident.

There were five more guests at table, but only a couple Kerry actually knew. Alderman and Mrs Frank Perry had been guests at Underwood on several occasions before her mother had died, and a couple of times since then. They had sent wreaths and letters of condolence on both occasions, and greeted her tonight with an obviously sincere declaration of how much her stepfather was missed by the town.

'A good man,' said the Alderman with a sad shake of his head. 'Many's the time I tried to persuade him to stand for council election, but he was never a man to push himself forward.'

Kerry could remember Andrew once mentioning the possibility and asking her what she thought about it. When she had said she thought he would make a very good councillor he had laughed and shaken his head, stating that local politics held no attractions for him. The world outside Sinclairs had held very few attractions those latter years.

'How about that son of his?' asked Mr Perry next, and she automatically stiffened. 'Is he home for good?'

'I'd say so,' she managed on a fairly level note. 'He gave up a very good job in America to take over here.'

'Not exactly take over, eh?' Mr Hall observed shrewdly from the top of the table. 'Larry tells me your stepfather divided his holdings equally between the two of you.'

'That's right,' Kerry confirmed with some reticence. 'It was just a figure of speech.'

'Except that Kerry has the sense to realise a man of his experience can obviously do a great deal for Sinclairs,' put in Larry smoothly. 'You'd get along with him, Uncle. To put it in the vernacular, he has his head screwed on t'reet way.'

The older man winced. 'If that's meant to be a Yorkshire accent I only hope you never take it into your head to do a dialect play. It's reyt, not reet!'

Larry was grinning. 'The schools I went to spent hours teaching me to speak properly.'

'Then you want to make sure your children keep some individuality. Half the pleasure in meeting new folk is trying to guess where they come from before being told.'

Kerry barely needed Larry's swift, smiling glance to tell her the significance of that simple-sounding statement. She had been accepted—a fit mother for the future generation of Halls. She didn't resent the trial she had been put to. Larry would one day inherit the whole works; it was only natural that his uncle should wish to make certain his chosen wife could comfortably cope with all her position in the community would entail.

There was frost on the ground when Larry took her home at eleven. He diverted along the road which skirted the golf course to park the car overlooking a miniature lake which formed a natural hazard at the seventeenth.

'I suppose I should wait for a more romantic setting,' he said against her hair a few moments later, 'but at least there's a moon. Kerry, you know what I'm going to say, don't you?'

'Yes,' she said, and felt him smile.

'Is that an answer or an acceptance?'

She drew a little away from him, trying to read his eyes in the semi-darkness. She said hesitantly, 'Would you still have wanted to marry me if your uncle hadn't give you the go-ahead?'

It was his turn to hesitate. 'There was never the least doubt in my mind that he'd think you were exactly right,' he came back at last.

'That wasn't what I asked.'

'I know it wasn't.' He gave a small resigned sigh. 'It

would have been difficult, Kerry, I don't mind admitting. My whole future is with Hall's Engineering. If I hadn't been so sure he'd like you I'd never have allowed myself to become as involved as I have.'

How wonderful, she thought wryly, to be in such command of one's emotions. She put up a hand and touched his cheek. 'It's all right, really. I just wanted you to be honest with me.'

'I'll always be honest with you.' He sounded relieved. 'We'll go and choose a ring tomorrow. Which stone do you prefer?'

'I'm not sure. You'll have to help me.' She felt as if someone else were saying the words for her. When he kissed her again she responded with a kind of desperation, running her hands inside his jacket over the smoothness of his shirt, slipping a button to slide the backs of her fingers down a chest equally devoid of hirsute appeal. His breathing became quicker and heavier and his own hands more demanding, hurting her breast in a caress which meant little beyond the immediate physical discomfort.

'Kerry,' he murmured. 'Oh God, darling, this is asking for trouble! You're so warm—so lovely and soft and warm!' He made a sudden abrupt movement, putting her away from him, sitting back in his own seat with a determined control. 'I'd better take you home while I still can. Making love now would be too risky when we only have to wait a few months.'

'Months?' Kerry queried in a voice she hardly recognised as hers. 'That long?'

'Well, five at least. A spring wedding would be ideal, don't you think?' He caught the quality in her silence and turned his head to look at her, tone softening. 'I know it isn't going to be easy for either of us, but it will be worth it in the end. We'll have the biggest, grandest wedding the town's seen in ages, followed by a honeymoon we'll remember the rest of our lives simply because we did wait.'

She said obliquely, 'What did you mean by risky?'

'Well, obviously . . .' He paused, expression undergoing a slight change. 'Kerry, you're not . . . taking anything, are you?'

'No.' She couldn't even summon indignation.

'Of course not.' He sounded apologetic. 'And you'll never have to. That's my department.'

'I thought you wanted children?'

'I do, but two's enough. I certainly wouldn't want a houseful.' He paused. 'Talking of houses, that plan you once had for turning Underwood into two separate residences might still be a pretty sound idea. It's certainly large enough for it, and it would be one way of getting round that condition your stepfather made about living there.'

'I'm not sure,' Kerry said carefully, 'that I'd want to go on living in Underwood. Couldn't we have a place of our own? What about your flat?'

'That's hardly big enough for two on a permanent basis.' His tone was disconcerted. 'And we'd be very fortunate to find a house with all Underwood's advantages. Land alone is at a premium these days. Why on earth . . .'

'Yes, I know.' The last thing she wanted was for him to ask her just why she was against the idea. 'It would be silly to leave a place like that, wouldn't it?'

'Especially when your stepfather so obviously wanted you to stay there and enjoy it.' He was patently relieved. 'We'll have to discuss it with Ross, of course, but I can't see him raising any objection. After all, he'll have his own half.'

Ross. The very sound of his name made her throat hurt. 'I'm tired,' she said dully. 'Take me home, please, Larry.'

'Your every wish is my command.' Smiling, he reached forward to switch on the ignition. 'I want you fresh for tomorrow's celebration. We'll go to Leeds for the ring, and spend the evening there. Dinner for two on a very special day. Sound nice?'

'Perfect.' To Kerry's ears the lack of enthusiasm was marked, but it appeared to satisfy him. She was being ridiculous. Everything Larry had said tonight made sense. Too much sense, a small voice whispered. Too well thought out for a spur-of-the-moment decision. In his own way he was probably as calculating as Ross.

They reached Underwood just before midnight to find a light still burning in the study.

'Ross is still up,' Larry observed on a note of satisfaction. 'That's good. We'll go and break the news. Don't suppose it will come as such a surprise to him.'

'Can't we leave it till tomorrow?' Kerry asked without moving, and he paused with a hand on the door to glance back at her.

'Why wait?'

'It's so late.'

'Not so much, and it won't take long. He should be the first to know. After all, he's your only family.'

'He's a Sinclair,' she said. 'I'm a Rendal.'

'But not for so much longer,' leaning back to kiss her fleetingly on the cheek. 'You're going to be a Hall, darling. Come on now.'

Ross came to the door of the study as they entered the house. He had taken off his suit jacket and tie and unfastened the collar of his shirt. The dark hair was roughed as if he might have run a hand through it recently. There was a certain weariness in the lines of his face.

'I was just about to have a nightcap,' he said. 'Join me?'

Larry answered for them both. 'That sounds just the job.'

Kerry wished it hadn't been the study. She sat down abruptly on the leather chesterfield, not looking at either

nan. Since hearing the will read all the pleasure had gone
›ut of this room for her.

Ross poured drinks and handed them round, lifting his
›wn glass in a brief gesture. 'Cheers.'

'Actually,' Larry said, 'we do have something to cele-
›rate.' His smile in Kerry's direction was already possessive.
'We're going to be married.'

There was so little reaction visible in the lean features
hat for a moment or two Kerry believed he had gone be-
'ond caring either way. Then he looked directly at her and
he saw the compression at the corners of his mouth, the
ool glint in his eyes. Even then she refused to believe him
apable.

'I see,' he said. 'Does your uncle approve?'

'All the way. He's very taken with her.'

'Aren't we all?' on a dry note. 'Would he still approve, do
ou think, if he knew she was coming to you second-hand?'

The silence seemed to last an age. Larry looked first un-
omprehending, then as realisation dawned his face went
tiff. 'What are you getting at?' he demanded.

Afterwards Kerry knew she had signed her own death
'arrant the moment she opened her mouth. Had she kept
alm and allowed Ross to answer before denouncing him
ıe might have stood a chance of having Larry believe her.
ut she didn't, because right then she couldn't.

'He's lying,' she exclaimed passionately. 'Whatever he
ells you, he's lying!'

Ross shrugged. 'He has a right to know about it, honey.
'ou should have told him yourself, then you start out fair
ıd square with no danger of someone else seeing fit to
pill the beans at a later date.'

'No one else knows!' she said, and saw the pitfall in that
atement in time to add swiftly, 'Because it never hap-
ened!' Her eyes went to Larry standing rigidly there with
e glass clutched in his hand. 'He threatened to do this

if I ever got serious about another man, only I never really thought he would. Can't you see ...'

'Another man.' Larry repeated the words slowly, changing the emphasis. 'Before there can be another, there has to be a first.'

'I didn't mean it like that!'

'Then how did you mean it? What reason would he have to threaten anything if it wasn't all true?'

She stared at him numbly, hardly able to credit what he was saying. 'You really believe it, don't you?' she whispered. 'His word against mine.'

If ever a man looked torn Larry did at that moment. 'All right,' he said at last, 'swear to me that it isn't true and I'll take your word.'

'Swear to you?' Sudden anger swept her, cutting through everything else like a scythe. 'I'll be damned if I will!'

'You'll be damned if you won't.' Ross shook his head, mouth curving in wry resignation. 'That stubborn streak of yours just won't let go, will it?' His glance came back to Larry. 'Look, I'm sorry about all this. Put it down to too close proximity. You can't throw two people together the way we were thrown without starting something. My father should have realised that himself.'

'Perhaps he did.' The tone was brittle. 'But I doubt if he intended this kind of relationship!'

'You mean he hoped we might marry?' He lifted his shoulders, mouth tilting. 'I suggested that some time ago, but Kerry didn't fancy the idea. Married to me she wouldn't have anything like the same freedom to please herself, and she knows it.'

The implication went home, that was obvious from the sudden dark flush which spread across the other's features. 'You've known I was seeing her for weeks,' he said shortly. 'Why didn't you stop it before things got this far?'

'I probably would have done if I'd realised the way things vere moving. You were both involved in the drama group, or one thing.'

'Not any more.' Kerry stood up, rigidly in control. 'You an go home happy, Larry, I've just resigned.'

'Happy?' He sounded anything but. 'I just don't under-tand how you could do this to me, Kerry. What am I going o tell my uncle?'

'Whatever you like. I really don't care. Now will you lease go.'

'Oh, I'll go all right!' He was angry himself now, be-vilderment giving way to self-righteousness. 'I suppose I hould be grateful for small mercies. I thought I was a good idge of character before tonight!' He put down the glass nd nodded stiffly to Ross. 'Thanks.'

'And there goes a broken man,' observed the latter sar-onically when the outer door had closed again. 'He's go-ng to have quite a job finding another candidate as minently suitable as you around Medfield.' He glanced at er when she failed to respond, brows lifting. 'No re-riminations?'

'I despise you,' she said low-toned. 'There's nothing low nough to call you!'

'True,' he agreed equably. 'On the other hand, you can't ay you weren't warned often enough. Amalgamation with Iall Engineering doesn't appeal.'

'And my feelings don't matter, of course.'

He smiled a little. 'If you want my honest opinion you're robably relieved to have the whole thing finished. Larry Iall was never your type. No man who has to ask approval efore he dares to propose to a girl is worth having. I doubt he could have satisfied you in any sense.'

'What makes you so sure he hasn't?' she flashed. 'Do you nagine you're the only man capable of making love to a oman?'

'No. Just the only one capable of making *you* forget any other considerations.'

'Maybe Larry could do that too.'

He shook his head tolerantly. 'No way. *I* know when you're lying, Kerry. You're not even very good at it.'

'No?' Her chin lifted. 'I was good at it the other night when you thought I was asleep. I didn't take any sleeping tablets. They were put there simply for effect!'

'You wouldn't have told me that,' he said after a moment. 'I wasted a lot of time on regrets.'

'You wouldn't know where to start regretting anything. You don't have a conscience!'

'But I do have the means of fetching you down off that soapbox.' His jaw was hard. 'Leave it, Kerry. It won't do either of us any good. Not that way.'

'Not any way. Nothing's changed.'

'Hasn't it? Gossip soon spreads. There'll have been enough speculation over the two of us already, you can bet.'

'Hardly, seeing you're rarely in the place.'

'I'm in it at nights, and that's when it counts in the eyes of those out looking for it. And who's to know how often I go out?'

'Sharon West perhaps?'

Surprise showed for an instant. 'You really do jump to conclusions, don't you?' he said.

'With good reason usually.' Kerry refused to allow doubt to infiltrate. 'Do you deny it?'

'I don't deny anything. It's a complete waste of time where you're concerned.' The pause was brief, his expression altering a fraction. 'Try thinking seriously about where we go from here. There are two alternatives. We either go on the way we are, which won't be easy, or you stop being so damned stubborn and make it legal.'

'I'd rather die first!'

His smile mocked. 'It's been called the small death—

something you wouldn't know about yet. You're going to marry me eventually, Kerry. You're going to have to.'

The urge to give in now and stop this whole charade was strong in her, but she resisted it. 'Unless I make over those shares to you first. Then there'd be no need. You'd have all the power you ever wanted.'

Something went out of the grey eyes. 'You'd still hold ten per cent.'

'So would the cousins, and their name isn't Sinclair either.'

'But they're unable to sell or will stock outside the Company by agreement, Dad forgot to place the same restriction on you.'

'He trusted me,' she said, 'which is more than you've ever done. There's no way I'd have given control of my stock to Larry.'

'I'm not going to argue the point. It's over and that's it. You didn't really want him anyway. Another man I might have felt sorry for, but I have a feeling friend Larry's pride took the brunt of the blow.' He paused, tone softer when he spoke again. 'Kerry ...'

'Oh, leave me alone,' she said wearily. 'You got what you wanted, now just leave me alone!'

'I can't leave you alone. We're stuck together in this house and we have to make the best of it.'

'That doesn't have to include making lies into truth.'

'Not even when everyone is going to believe them the truth anyhow?'

She shook her head emphatically. 'Larry won't spread that story around. He wouldn't like it known that he was fooled into proposing to me.'

'He'll have to give his uncle some convincing reason for his sudden change of mind. The proposal may never reach outside ears, but you can safely bet the rest will. The only way you're going to be able to walk round this town, or the Store either for that matter, without being aware of the whispers is to take all the spice out of the story. People might sniff and say "about time too", but a marriage certificate nullifies a lot of sins. We could make a good job of it if we both worked at it hard enough.'

It was a moment or two before Kerry spoke. When she did it was with a flat intonation. 'I'm tired, Ross. I'm going to bed.'

'All right, we'll talk about it again over the weekend. I'll be going in the Store in the morning, but you sleep in and get some rest ready for the evening.' His gaze silenced her protest before it was born. 'We have to go. It's expected of us. Don't worry, there won't have been time for any gossip to have spread.'

'Gossip you'll have caused,' she stated bitterly, and saw his mouth firm.

'If you're waiting for me to say I'm sorry, you'll have a long wait. I'd have done worse to keep you out of friend Larry's avaricious hands. See you around lunchtime. Is Mrs Payne coming in?'

Kerry nodded, not trusting herself to speak.

'Good. She'll be retiring in a couple of months according to what she was saying the other day. We'll have to see about getting someone to live in and take over all the housekeeping duties if you intend carrying on at the Store. There's the flat over the garage which only needs doing up again.'

This time the words were jerked from her. 'You're taking too much for granted.'

'No, I'm not. You'll see.' He smiled. 'Go on to bed. Tomorrow's another day.'

Kerry went, too numb to think straight. Sleep was what she wanted and needed: a few hours' respite from all problems. Somewhat surprisingly she found it almost as soon as her head touched the pillow.

CHAPTER EIGHT

MRS PAYNE was vacuuming the drawing room when Kerry got down at ten, the radio going full blast.

'I've done t' sitting room and t' study,' she announced, switching off the machine and lifting her voice above the blare of pop music. 'Want any breakfast?'

Kerry shook her head. 'Just coffee, and I can get that myself. Would you like some?'

'No, thanks. Just had a cuppa tea.'

Kerry hesitated, wondering if what she wanted to ask was worth the effort of raising her voice so far. Finally, she went over and turned down the radio by way of compromise.

'I hear you're thinking of leaving in a little while?' she said.

'That's right.' The tone was matter-of-fact. 'I'll be sixty-six in a couple of months. Thought I might give myself a birthday present. Got a bit of a nest-egg tucked away for a rainy day, thanks to Mr Sinclair, and it'd be nice to put my feet up of an afternoon for a change.'

'I'm sure it would,' Kerry said warmly. 'You don't look sixty-six.'

'Times when I feel eighty, love. If you'll be needing a replacement for me there's somebody I can recommend.'

'Actually,' Kerry said a little awkwardly, 'I think Ross will want someone willing to live in. There's the flat over the garage and . . .'

The other face held a sudden eager anticipation. 'If that's case, my son Billy's getting married soon to this young woman I just spoke about. She's a widow—no kids—

and a grand cook! They don't have a place to live yet because her house was rented and she had to get out. She'd suit you down t' ground.' She gave Kerry no time to comment, perhaps sensing doubt. 'My Billy's a gardener,' she added. 'Works for t' recreation department—you know, parks and gardens and such. Anyway, he'd be more than willing to lend a hand round t' grounds here in his spare time. Old Aden Baxter's getting a bit past looking after it properly on his own.'

Kerry could agree with that, not that it was the man's fault. No way could his dismissal after so many years' service be countenanced, yet it had been obvious for some time that something was going to have to be done. This could very well be the ideal solution to both problems. Fleetingly, she wished her own personal ones could be solved as easily.

'It sounds just the thing,' she admitted. 'Of course, the flat has to be got ready. It hasn't been used except for storage since before I came here.'

'Bless you, give 'em a bit of paint and paper and they'll be happy to do t' decorating themselves. Probably like to, seeing as how they'd be living in t' place.'

'Supposing they started a family?' Kerry asked diffidently. 'The flat is large enough for two, but it would be a tight squeeze with any more than that.'

'Doubt it now. They're both gone forty.' She chuckled. 'Takes his time looking, does our Billy, before he does any choosing. Can I tell him?'

'Well, I'd have to mention it to Ross first, but he'll be home before you leave, I think. I'm sure he'll be in complete agreement. It really couldn't have worked out better!' She stopped there, colouring a little. 'Not that we shan't be sorry to lose you, of course.'

The chuckle came again. 'Don't look so stricken, love. I'm getting past it as well. Dad's going to enjoy having all his meals got ready at proper time instead of having to wait till I get home. Mind you, he's never objected to me coming up here. Bought us things we wouldn't have got without. We can manage comfortably, though, now all t' kids are gone. Thought we'd never get rid of our Billy, though. Just shows you it's never too late.'

She could perhaps use that as her own philosophy, reflected Kerry wryly as she went through to the kitchen. It wasn't too late to accept what Ross was offering and make the best of it. He might even one day learn to love her the way she loved him—regardless of anything and everything. And if he didn't—well, that was something she would have to learn to accept. At least she had more hold over him than Margot had had.

He arrived home around one, sniffing the air appreciatively when he came in. 'Something smells good,' he observed as Kerry came out from the dining room. The pause held a question. 'Special occasion?'

'Mrs Payne thinks it is. She cooked her best coq-au-vin.' The tension was still there despite her attempt to act normally. 'I'll tell you why over lunch.'

He received the news with immediate approval. 'Couldn't have worked out better,' he said. 'In fact it mightn't be a bad idea to offer—Billy, did you say?—a full-time job. The grounds are starting to look really tatty, even allowing for winter.'

'What about Aden Baxter?' she asked on a note of concern. 'We can't just tell him to go.'

'I wouldn't attempt it. They can both work together providing it's realised it's on an equal basis. It won't matter too much then when old Baxter feels like taking a day off occasionally.'

Kerry kept her head down as she said, 'You can be quite compassionate when you want to be, can't you?'

'Is it compassion? I thought it was common sense.

There's always been too much work here for one anyway. When Baxter finally gives up we can find another part-timer to help out.'

She looked up then to meet his quizzical regard, feeling her heart start its familiar upward beat. 'Anything special crop up this morning?' she asked quickly.

'Nothing worth dwelling on.' He waited a moment, then said with deliberation, 'Did you think about what I said last night?'

'Yes.' Her voice was low.

'And?'

It was difficult to speak through the tightness in her throat. 'I've decided I will marry you—if that's what you really want.'

'That's what I really want.' There was no note of triumph in his voice, just a quiet satisfaction. He pushed back his chair from the table, added softly, 'Come here, Kerry.'

She looked back at him blindly before complying, to be drawn down on to his knees and held securely while he kissed her. His hand was in her hair, cupping the back of her head, his mouth gentle yet not far from passion. When Mrs Payne walked into the room he made no attempt to let her go, holding her where she was to smile at the older woman.

'You can be first to congratulate us, Mrs Payne. We're getting married.'

'It's all happening, isn't it?' she responded, showing little surprise. 'I must say, Mr Sinclair would have been pleased!'

'Do you really think so?' Kerry asked, unaware of the eager need in the question.

'Oh yes, I'm sure so. He said as much once before Mr Ross went away. Always had his plans, did Mr Sinclair.' She beamed on them both. 'Fancy any pudding?'

Ross laughed. 'Wheel it in. My appetite is almost back to Yorkshire standards!'

'Not by a long chalk,' came the derisive snort. 'You neither of you eat enough to keep a fly alive! It's apple pie and cream. I'll fetch it.'

'And that should put an effective stop to any rumours,' Ross remarked with satisfaction. 'Our friend there will have anybody by the throat who tries it on near her.'

'Is that all that bothers you?' Kerry asked, and he smiled and shook his head.

'No, but it bothers you. It took emotional blackmail to get you to say yes to me. As I said last night, I'm not going to apologise for it.'

'I wouldn't expect you to apologise for anything,' she said. 'It isn't your style.'

'And you accept it that way?'

'I don't have any choice.' She hesitated, making herself meet the grey eyes. 'Ross, I hope you're not going to expect everything at once. I mean . . .'

'I know what you mean.' He studied her with an unreadable expression. 'If you want me to wait until we're married, it's going to have to be soon. How about next week? We could take a cruise for a honeymoon and miss this lousy weather. South America, I think, this time of year.'

'What about the Store?' she asked with uncertainty.

'What about the Store? Everything is in hand. Nothing much for me to do until the New Year anyway.' He kissed her lightly again. 'You'd enjoy a cruise. We could extend it over Christmas if you liked. Christmas in Rio?'

He was going too fast for her; she needed time to consider. 'The party,' she said quickly. 'I've already asked people to the party.'

'From the drama group?'

'Yes.' The acknowledgement was wry. 'Not being a member any more I suppose it can be counted as off. Jill will be disappointed.'

'Jill?'

'The girl who was batting her eyelashes at you the night you came home.'

Ross smiled dryly. 'Afraid I didn't notice. I was too busy planning what I was going to do to you when I got you on your own.' He paused, searching her face. 'Can we put all that behind us now?'

'Yes.' It wouldn't be immediate, she knew, but there was little else she could say. She made a jerky movement as the door opened to admit Mrs Payne again, embarrassed to be caught still in the same position.

'Don't mind me,' the newcomer said cheerfully. 'With three lasses, I've been through it all before.' She put down the tray, gave them both another cheery twinkle and added, 'I'll leave you to help yourselves.'

Kerry escaped Ross's restraining hands before she got to the door, taking her seat again a little breathlessly. 'Oh, Mrs Payne, it's all right about the flat. You can tell Billy and his fiancée tonight.'

'Perhaps they'd like to come up and see us tomorrow while we're all free,' Ross suggested easily. 'I'm hoping I can interest your son in a permanent job. Do you think there might be a possibility?'

'Wouldn't be a bit surprised—if t' money's right.'

'I'm sure we could come to a satisfactory arrangement. Baxter would be staying on while he can still manage it, but I think this winter is starting to get him down already.'

'Aye, and he won't be on his own!' She smiled happily. 'It would be grand to have our Billy living here. They'd neither of them let you down, Mr Ross.'

'I'm sure of it. Tomorrow, then. Make it around three.'

The apple pie was delicious; it always was. Kerry toyed with hers for several minutes before finally putting down her spoon. 'I'm not really all that hungry,' she said.

Ross had finished first. Now he reached for the coffee pot. 'I see you've even got Mrs P. trained to the earthenware,' he observed. 'Black or white?'

'White, please. And I should be doing that.'

'Does it really matter?' He slid her cup across. 'We don't have to be at the town hall until sevenish. What would you like to do this afternoon?'

'Anything,' she said. 'I don't mind. You say.'

He shook his head. 'What I'd like you won't go along with. No, I'm not complaining. Well, not too much. I can wait a week—just.'

'A week is far too soon,' she protested softly.

'No, it isn't. Not in our circumstances. We don't have anybody to please but ourselves. The *Empress* leaves Southampton on Friday for a six-week cruise to the Canaries and across to Brazil. We could be married Friday morning and go straight down.'

'How do you know they still have berths going spare?'

'Because they're still advertising in this morning's paper. Cook's will deal with the reservations for me. Just a phone call is all that's needed.'

'I couldn't possibly be ready by Friday,' she said. 'I don't have the right clothes, for one thing.'

'There's a whole store to choose from, and Leeds is just an hour away if you can't find what you want at Sinclairs.' His lips firmed. 'No more excuses. I'm going to get those reservations sorted out.'

Kerry sat still as he went from the room, trying to sort herself out. South America for Christmas—more important, South America with Ross. Six weeks away from Sinclairs and all it meant for both of them. Six weeks in which to simply be together. Surely that was worth a little rushing around. She suddenly and desperately hoped he could get those reservations.

It seemed an age before he came back. He was smiling, she saw with relief.

'All set,' he said. 'We got the last stateroom on "A" deck.

I said I'd go into town this afternoon and let them have a cheque. Feel like coming with me?'

Kerry shook her head. 'I'd rather not, if you don't mind.'

'Scared of seeing Larry?'

'Not scared so much as uncomfortable. He was going to take me for a ring today.'

'Which is something we still have to do.' He registered her expression with comprehension. 'Did you think you wouldn't be getting one? It might be a short engagement, but it's going to have all the trappings. We could choose your wedding ring at the same time. I hope you don't expect me to wear one too. That's like putting a ring through a bull's nose.'

She said, 'You mean you'd rather appear unattached.'

'Hey!' His tone was soft. 'Don't go reading too much into too little. It was meant to be a joke. You're going to have to learn to trust me, Kerry. What's past is past.'

So many words, she thought, and none the one she wanted so desperately to hear. If he would just once tell her he loved her, even if he didn't really mean it, everything would be all right.

'Just tell me one thing,' she said. '*Have* you been seeing Sharon West these last weeks?'

'Not outside business hours,' he stated levelly. And don't ask any more questions, that contraction of his jawline said for him. 'We're going into town,' he added on a decisive note. 'You're going to be wearing that ring tonight.'

'You're not thinking of making any announcement?' she asked in alarm.

'It won't be needed. Those who see it will guess, and those who don't will soon hear.' Ross glanced at his watch. 'It's gone two now. If we can't find what we want in Medfield, we'll have to leave it till Monday and go into Leeds. Raynors should be able to show you a good selection.'

For Kerry the whole expedition was both ordeal and intoxication rolled into one. The travel agency was expecting them and had brochures and other literature to hand ready. They promised to have all documentation through by the following Wednesday. Raynors was almost exactly oposite. The best jewellers in Medfield, it provided a selection of stones more than adequate to Kerry's desires. With both Ross's and the assistant's help she finally chose a solitaire diamond she privately thought cost far too much, but which suited her finger admirably. For a wedding ring she picked a plain wide band, her heart turning over as the assistant slid it on for her.

Pouring tea for them both in the foyer of the Royal Hotel, she was highly conscious of the flashing stone, turning her hand a little so that it would catch the light.

'It's beautiful,' she said, catching Ross watching her. 'I'm going to be scared stiff of losing it.'

'It's insured,' he said. 'We're going to have to look nippy if we're going to make the reception.'

She glanced at him uncertainly, sensing something in him which jarred with the occasion, but there was nothing to be read from the lean features. 'We'll make it,' she said. 'It won't take so long to get ready.'

'It won't take me long, admittedly.' The smile was back in his eyes. 'I was thinking about you. I've yet to meet the woman who can doll herself up for anything in less than a couple of hours.'

Kerry was the first to break the small silence, her voice bright. 'There are exceptions to every rule. I bet I'm ready before you.'

'Done.' The glint was not wholly amusement. 'But if I win I'll demand a forfeit.'

They got back to the house before six. Kerry had already put out the dress she intended wearing, together with fresh underwear and narrow-thonged gold sandals. Twenty minutes later, showered, made up and dressed, she ran a final smoothing hand over her hair and stood back to view herself critically in the long mirror. The dress was a deep creamy beige silk jersey which fitted down to her hips, then swirled into graceful folds to the floor, its neckline high and cowled, the gold plaited belt worn loosely knotted medieval fashion.

There was a tap on the door. 'Ready or not,' Ross called, 'I'm coming in.'

She turned to face him as he did so, seeing his eyes light appreciatively as he ran them over her.

'You look beautiful,' he said. He came closer, a smile touching his lips. 'No bra? What will the elders think?'

'I can't,' she said. 'I don't have one which doesn't show under this.' She glanced down at herself with faint concern, self-consciousness forgotten for the moment. 'Do you think I should wear something else?'

'And ruin my evening?' He laughed and shook his head. 'You'll probably find few of the men looking you in the eye tonight, but it's only the wives who'll be complaining.'

'But that's just it, isn't it?' taking him seriously. 'I shouldn't be attracting that kind of attention.'

This time the shake of his head was almost indulgent. 'Kerry, we own the damned Store. Within reason we act the way it suits us to act. You've no standards to meet except your own.'

She looked at him for a moment. 'And yours.'

'You always topped them,' he said. 'No more uncertainty. You're going to be a Sinclair, and the Sinclairs are never uncertain—even when they're in the wrong.'

'Amen,' she responded with feeling, and saw his eyes glint before he took her in his arms.

'We're going to be late,' he murmured a few moments later, still holding her. 'At least once we're on that ship we don't have to answer to any call. They'll know we're on honeymoon—they always guess. We'll be left strictly to our own devices for at least the first week.'

'I'll have to put on some more lipstick,' Kerry said unsteadily. 'And you've messed up my hair again.'

'Complaints, complaints!' But he was smiling. 'At least you weren't thinking about your hair while I was doing the mussing. I'll go and get the car started.'

Sinclairs' top management were waiting in an aloof little group close by the Town Hall's outer doors. Resplendent in purple taffeta, Beryl Gregson was the first to spot their arrival, nudging her husband with a force which almost knocked his sherry glass out of his hand. The whole group moved as one to enclose them in a protective phalanx, not exactly fawning but certainly eager to claim the privilege of close association.

Shaking hands with Mrs Gregson whom she saw once a year, Kerry was aware that her ring had been noticed from the sudden widening of the other's eyes. A moment later she saw the lady whispering to one of the other wives, who immediately took a surreptitious look for herself. By the time they sat down to dinner, she calculated, the news would probably have travelled throughout the room. There would be speculation, of course. Was it Ross or someone else? But if someone else why wasn't he here with her tonight? If they got through the evening without someone giving way under the strain and asking outright, they would be fortunate. Yet why not? They had to know some time, and any interest generated tonight would be as nothing compared with Friday's news.

Friday. It didn't seem possible that she was going to marry Ross in less than a week. Looking at him now, devastating in the stark black and white, she still couldn't make herself believe it. Earlier in her bedroom, he had once more underlined the physical need he had of her, and that was something to cling to. For the present her own deeper emotions would have to suffice for both of them.

As staff occasions went, this one had to be called a howling success. Once the formalities of the meal were over, Ross himself caused an immediate relaxation in protocol by going out to the bar and buying a first drink for all those present. Within minutes he had the younger element chatting freely, leaning an elbow on the wall behind him as his glance roved from one face to another. Stuck with the Gregsons and Fieldings on the far side of the room, Kerry waited for a convenient moment before excusing herself politely and going to join him.

'We were discussing staff reorganisation,' he said over the small silence which fell on her appearance, and she pulled a face.

'Not shop, tonight of all nights!'

'It wasn't Mr Sinclair who started it, Miss Rendal,' proffered one of the young men standing by. 'We did. We're all interested in what's happening to Sinclairs.'

'The wind of change,' Kerry acknowledged, and heard no dry note in her voice. She smiled at the speaker. 'Haven't we met before?'

He blushed faintly, looking suddenly uncomfortable. 'Didn't think you'd remember,' he muttered, and then on a bolder note, 'I asked you to dance once a few dinners back, but Mr Sinclair—old Mr Sinclair—said no. It was only a dare.'

'Why don't you ask her again?' Ross suggested easily. 'The disco's going full strength already by the sound of it.'

Kerry took her cue at once. 'I'd like that. It's ages since I had the chance to let my hair down.'

'Oh, well, in that case——' the grin made him look boyish—'may I have the pleasure?'

Laughing, she accompanied him through the double swing doors which only partially deadened the blare from within, aware of her former companions' disapproving glances and suddenly not caring a whit. There were plenty of people already on the floor, and it was too dark for her identity to cause any stir, except among those closest to the pair of them as they joined in the gyrations.

Feeling her body slowly loosen up to the beat, Kerry realised she was enjoying herself in a way she hadn't done for years. She had mixed with older people for so long she had begun to feel more their generation than her own. Even Larry had failed to make her feel really young, probably because he himself was old before his time. Twenty-four hours ago she had been sitting there in his uncle's house waiting approval. Thank heaven Ross had stepped in —regardless of the way he had done it. To think it might have been Larry's ring she was wearing tonight! The very notion made her go chilly inside. She smiled brightly at her companion to counteract it.

'You certainly can move!' he shouted admiringly, coming closer so that she would hear him. 'You're dead different!'

From what? Kerry wondered humorously. But she knew what he meant. Different from what he had expected—different from the image which filtered down from the top floor. Upper and lower management were poles apart, never mind the minor grades.

The music changed after a few minutes, slowing to a medley of modern ballads which had most couples moving closer to one another. Kerry's partner hesitated only briefly before moving up to slide both arms round her waist, not holding her too close but obviously not prepared to stand on ceremony either, now that the ice was broken. She put her hands on his shoulders as most of the other girls were doing with their partners, and relaxed into the one/two/feet together progression which catered for everything outside of beat tempo.

'Can I ask you a personal question?' he queried boldly a moment or two later.

Taken aback, but sensing what was coming, she gave a smile. 'You can ask. I might not be prepared to answer.'

'It's nothing bad,' he hastened to assure her. 'Just that ... well, somebody said that you and Mr Sinclair were engaged, that's all.'

She tried to make it sound matter-of-fact. 'They were right. We are. It only happened yesterday, which is why there's been no announcement of any kind.'

'How about that?' He sounded delighted—probably, Kerry reflected dryly, because he was the first to verify the rumour.

'What do you really think to all the changes at Sinclairs?' she asked swiftly before he could progress a stage further on his fact-finding mission.

'Oh, great!' The enthusiasm was unfeigned. 'It's a good firm to work for, but it's always been a bit stuffy.' He caught himself up, looked at her, then grinned again. 'Well, it has.'

'I agree with you. We got in a bit of a rut.'

'How far's it going to go?' he asked, emboldened by her attitude. 'Nobody's sure—not in the sports department anyway.'

'Oh, as far as it can, I'd say.' She had said it before thinking about it, yet having said it was like releasing a load from her mind. 'It's all up to the Chairman. He's the expert.'

'He's great!' It seemed to be both his favourite adjective and biggest accolade together. 'Old Mr Sinclair was okay too, of course, but we didn't see much of him.'

He wasn't so old either, she wanted to say, but she refrained. 'Old' was a state of mind—an impression given. It had little to do with years.

Ross was still with the same crowd when they went back. He lifted a mocking eyebrow at her before detaching himself from the group with an ease she envied.

'Enjoy yourselves,' he said. 'The night's still young.'

'I think we'd better go and pay some attention to the top table lot,' Kerry murmured as they moved away together. 'They're looking rather put out.'

'We were with them all through dinner,' Ross returned, sounding distinctly unmoved. He glanced at her, then shrugged and smiled. 'Okay, I suppose you're right. The dancing's started in the other place. I'll ask Mrs Gregson, for my sins.'

The evening began to run together after that. Kerry danced with Mr Gregson once and then later with Arthur Fielding, finding the going heavy in both cases, and not only where the steps were concerned. At one point she saw her former partner standing in the doorway with a couple of others about the same age, and couldn't resist the urge to make a wry grimace over Arthur's shoulder as they came level, to have it promptly returned.

She only danced once with Ross, and that for a mere five minutes before the particular session of dances ended. It was quite a lot later when she saw him take Sharon West on to the floor, the latter drifting into his arms as if she were made for them. Ross seemed to enjoy the contact too, judging from the way he held her. Kerry turned away with twin spots of colour burning faintly on her cheekbones. Did he really have to do this to her tonight of all nights? He had denied any kind of outside relationship with Sharon only this afternoon, yet appearances right now would suggest a very close one.

From then on the evening was simply something to be got through. She had never been more thankful for the finish of it around one. During the leavetakings Ross was right there at her elbow, but she sensed something in him that had not been there before.

At long last they were outside in the crisp, frosty air, and he was putting her into the Jaguar already brought round from the car park at the rear. As she waited for him to come round to his own seat she caught a glimpse of her late disco partner coming down the steps, his gaze on the silvery blue machine with a wistful expression, and suddenly wished she were one of that laughing, chattering crowd heading for late night transport from the town centre. She'd been living in a dream world believing she could cope with the knowledge that Ross didn't care deeply enough for her. She wanted everything—or nothing.

He didn't say a word all the way home, confirming her suspicion that his mind was elsewhere. She went indoors first while he put the car away, heading straight upstairs for her room and firmly closing the door. Let him puzzle out for himself why she hadn't bothered to wait to say goodnight—if he didn't already know.

She was already half undressed when he came upstairs; she heard him because she was listening for it. Instead of turning to the right along his own stretch of corridor, his footsteps came right along to her door. Kerry snatched up the recently discarded dress and held it up against her as the door opened abruptly.

'Don't you dare walk in here like that!' she snapped at him. 'We're not married yet!'

'It may be as well until we've cleared one or two matters up,' he came back on a grim note. 'I'm not going to spend my life avoiding all other women just to save trouble with you!'

'It wasn't just *any* woman, was it?'

'No, it was an old friend, I dance for ten minutes with an old friend, and come off the floor to an atmosphere you could cut with a knife.'

'You're more than friends,' she came back bitingly, and saw his lips twist.

'Correction—we *were* more than friends. A long time ago. You were still at school, if I remember. Hardly adequate competition.'

'My instincts were developed enough to detest you.'

'So I recall. It's an unfortunate age, fifteen. Betwixt and between. Nine years made a lot more difference then, I admit. To me you were just a kid.' He paused before adding hardily, 'Tonight you acted like one again.'

'Sharon and Margot,' she said with brittle inflection. 'And how many more?'

'What would you like, a written list? We were supposed to be forgetting the past.'

'How can I forget it when I keep getting it thrown in my face? Would you like to discover *I'd* had previous affairs?'

'No,' he admitted. 'We've already agreed it's a selfish attitude, but that's the way it is. We see sexual relationships from different angles. You want a ring on your finger and both our names on a piece of paper before you indulge. Well, okay, that's what you're getting, but few men are either willing or able to stay celibate till the right one comes along—not unless they happen to meet very early on in life.'

The anger had gone from her, but not the pain. 'I'm not sure I am the right one for you,' she said on a husky note. 'It's just sexual with us, isn't it?'

'Meaning I'm only marrying you because I can't have you any other way?' There was irony in his voice. 'You're forgetting Sinclairs.'

'No, I'm not. I can't forget it. But I doubt if you'd have been willing to tie yourself down to someone you didn't even feel physical attraction towards. It isn't enough, Ross. Not for me it isn't.'

'You haven't given me the chance to make it enough,' he came back roughly. 'But it's going to have to be. You're not backing out of it now, Kerry. You've got my ring on your finger, and on Friday you'll have another. That still applies no matter what happens between now and then, so you've nothing to lose by letting me settle at least some of your doubts right now.'

Her mouth tilted wryly. 'A moment or two ago you were furious with me, and now you want to take me to bed.'

'That's how it goes. Holding that damned dress up in front of you like that is provocation enough.'

'I'm not trying to provoke you,' she said. 'That's why I'm not putting it down.' Her chest felt tight. 'Please go, Ross. I'll try to remember about those different angles in future.'

His shrug held resignation. 'Have it your own way. See you in the morning.' He made no attempt even to kiss her, turning back to the door.

So that was that, Kerry reflected numbly when she was alone again. On Friday she would be Ross's wife. She could still get out of it, of course: nobody could force someone to marry them. But what other reasonable solution was there? They certainly could not go on living together like this any longer. She would just have to learn to accept things as they were, and hope that time would bring them closer together. Time—and a little more effort on her part perhaps. Ross wasn't going to change now. It was she who was going to have to do the changing.

CHAPTER NINE

BILLY PAYNE and his wife-to-be, Sheila, came to see them on the Sunday afternoon as arranged. Within half an hour it was all settled. Billy was to leave the Council and begin immediately, while Sheila would take over from her future mother-in-law in five weeks' time when she herself would also be Mrs Payne. In the meantime there was the flat to be prepared. Both expressed delight at the look of the place, despite its present appearance.

'Soon have it shipshape,' Billy stated with confidence, refusing Ross's offer of professional help. 'I've done all my mother's paper-hanging and painting, so there's no trouble there. All I'll need is materials.'

'And I'm so glad it isn't furnished,' Sheila confided to Kerry a little diffidently. 'I've a cartload of furniture in storage. I can pick out all my favourite pieces and get rid of what we can't use.'

'Nice couple,' Ross commented when they had gone. 'It'll have to be either Mr Payne or Billy, though. No way can I go calling a man that size Billy!'

Kerry laughed. 'I think it's probably only his mother who calls him that. To her he's still a son rather than a grown man.' She paused, giving him an oblique glance. 'Do you remember your mother very well, Ross?'

'Fairly. She was a very quiet, very gentle person—never very strong. I don't think she ever completely recovered from my birth.' His tone was reflective, his gaze on the leaping dance of flame in the sitting room hearth. 'I can remember thinking how different she and Dad were—two complete opposites. Your mother was much more able to cope with him.'

She said softly, 'Do you still think she married him for his money?' and saw the dark head swing towards her, his expression wry.

'I wasn't much of a diplomat at twenty-two, was I? I suppose basically I resented the whole idea of his marrying again at all. Actually, I became pretty fond of her. I was cut up about the accident.'

'So much so you couldn't be bothered to come over for the funeral?' She had to say it; it had been festering for too long.

Ross looked back at her steadily. 'I wanted to come, Kerry. I rang Dad and told him I was coming. He said unless I was prepared to come home for good on his terms there was no point in my coming at all.'

Kerry drew in a long, slow breath, a weight seeming to fall from her. 'I'm sorry, Ross. All this time I've been thinking you just didn't care enough to make the effort.'

'Hardly surprising.' His tone was dry. 'He got his own way, didn't he? I came back on his terms.'

'Not quite,' she said. 'I'm not going to block you any more over Sinclairs. Do what has to be done to make it profitable again. We might lose a few old customers, but you're right, you can't run a business on sentiment. Only Ross ...' she hesitated, reluctant to dim the warmth in his eyes ... 'you won't make it too soulless, will you?'

'It won't be soulless at all,' he promised. 'You'll see.' He got up and came over to where she sat on the sofa, drawing her to her feet. 'It's going to make all the difference.'

Not to his emotions, she thought as he gathered her to him. He still couldn't tell her he loved her. Yet what had she expected? One couldn't buy love; it had to be earned And she would earn it, she really would. One day he would say those three little words to her and mean it with everything in him. She had to believe that or nothing was worthwhile.

Kate Anthony brought in a huge envelope around tea-time on Monday, handing it to Kerry with a smile of amusement.

'One of the sales staff asked me to let you have it,' she said. 'From the sports department, I think.'

The card was an Image Arts, Razzamatazz Twenties showing two cherub doll figures, appropriately dressed, standing at a bar with glasses raised in an attitude suggestive of a fair degree of inebriation. The male figure was carrying a gangster type tommygun and wore a king-sized leer, while the female was looking sideways at him in coy invitation. Over the top in big, bold letters it said: Congratulations. Inside were a dozen or more signatures, all with various departmental names at the side. Heading the list was a carefully executed 'Dave Rawson' from Sports who had to be her partner from Saturday evening. The others, she realised, must be the gang Ross had been drinking with while she and Dave danced.

'Isn't that great of them to go to all that trouble!' she exclaimed, laughing again at the illustration. 'Cheeky devils!'

Kate had a look and put on a disapproving expression although her eyes were twinkling. 'I think it's meant to be rather suggestive,' she said.

'I'm sure of it.' Kerry took it back and stood it on the edge of her desk, aware that the news was certainly no secret anywhere in the store by now. 'It should be interesting to watch reactions.'

Kate waited until she had sat down again before observing evenly, 'You know, a few weeks ago I'd never have said you and Mr Sinclair were going to get along at all, much less be married. I remember coming into the Chairman's office that day and finding you both there. If you'll excuse me saying so, you looked anything but thrilled to have him home.'

'A lot can happen in a few weeks,' Kerry said lightly,

and was thankful that the other was unaware just how much had. 'We don't have any family to please—except the Baratts, of course—so there's no reason to wait.' She had already told the secretary about Friday's plans, with the injunction to keep it quiet for the present. 'Anyway,' she added by way of additional rationalisation, 'we want to be back before the real upheaval starts.'

'Yes, it's going to be quite hectic for a few months, I imagine.' The comment was not altogether disconsolate. 'Things certainly started happening when Mr Sinclair arrived!'

Kate went out again soon afterwards. On impulse, Kerry thumbed the switch on the intercom for Ross's office.

'Are you free?' she asked. 'I have something to show you.'

'Sure,' he said. 'Come on through.'

He was vastly amused by the card. 'Bet it was your long-standing admirer's idea,' he said. 'He looked capable. I'll do the acknowledging for both of us.'

'You're not going to tick them off, are you?'

'Not at all. On the other hand, we have to observe some elements of protocol. Too much encouragement and you'll have him up here with flowers before you know it!'

'Only if he could disguise them as something else,' she retorted dryly. 'I've yet to hear of a Yorkshire man buying flowers for any woman! I think most of you would rather die than be caught carrying a bouquet.'

'You could be right.' He leaned back in his chair studying her, the smile still lingering about his lips. 'Are you planning to carry flowers yourself on Friday?'

'If I do it will only be a couple of roses, or something similar.' She paused before adding levelly, 'I think I might go into Leeds for everything I want, Ross. If I start shopping here word is going to get round.'

'And speculation start running riot.' He shrugged. 'It's

going to start doing that anyway once it's known we got married so soon. Put on a few pounds and you'll have the pundits saying "I told you so".'

'Is this another of your arguments against waiting till Friday?' Kerry asked a little coolly, and the smile came back.

'It wasn't, but it could be. Are you weakening?'

'No.'

'Shame.' His tone was light, the pause brief. 'Why not take a couple of days and go down to London? The choice might be greater at this time of the year.'

'Overnight?' The question was too abrupt; she saw that from his expression.

'One night less for me to have to control my premature urges.'

So far as she was concerned, at least, Kerry reflected, and was immediately ashamed of the cynicism. Ross was right, she couldn't go through life suspecting every move he made.

'It might not be a bad idea,' she said, eager to cancel out the momentary unpleasantness. 'I could take the eight-forty tomorrow morning and come back by the three-fifty Wednesday afternoon.'

'Fine.' He sounded easy again. 'By the way, I told Mrs Payne not to bother preparing anything for tonight. We'll go out to dinner.'

He took her to the station next morning, coming on to the platform to see her off.

'Try and fit in a show tonight,' he said. 'It would make a change.'

Sitting back as the train drew out of the station, Kerry wondered wryly if he had meant the remark as a spur to her memory. Since Friday she had neither seen nor heard from Larry, and didn't expect to do so, unless by accident. She was going to miss the group, and Wednesday rehearsals, but there was no other way round it. As soon as she got back she would send in her resignation, and leave it to Larry to do any explaining he thought necessary. He would have to say something anyway when she failed to turn up tomorrow night.

It was gone noon by the time she reached her London hotel. After checking in, she left her case to be unpacked later and just had a quick brush-up before setting out again. Lunch would have to be a quick affair if she were to get a reasonable time around the shops. In the end she settled for a sandwich and coffee, promising herself a more elaborate spread at dinner.

She enjoyed the afternoon, finding added incentive in the knowledge that she was choosing clothes with a view to Ross's approval. A fairly conservative dresser by nature, she found herself now trying on garments which at one time would not have drawn a second glance simply because she thought Ross would find them appealing. One particularly figure-hugging swimsuit with matching silk skirt and jacket she bought in two different shades because she couldn't decide which she liked best, shrugging off the extravagance on the thought that this was a once-in-a-lifetime event—the marriage at least.

Apart from cruise clothes, she also bought lots of new lingerie, revelling in the idea of starting new from the skin outwards. The filmy, floaty nightdresses and negligés were more than she could resist. She could imagine sitting at breakfast in their stateroom wearing one of these—appropriately made up and with hair just right, of course. Thank goodness she didn't have to wear rollers at night! What on earth did women who did do?

She didn't get back to the hotel until six-fifteen after trying half an hour to get a taxi, collapsing on to the bed with a vow to take things a little easier in the morning. She had brought along a second suitcase into which to put her purchases, and would deposit both in the left luggage before proceeding with the smaller items she still had to buy. In the meantime, she had this evening to get through. She wished Ross could be here with her right now. It was too early to phone him; he probably wouldn't be home yet. On the other hand, it was really too late to start thinking about a show. By the time she had arranged about a ticket and got ready she wouldn't have time to eat, and she was hungry. No, dinner right here in the hotel restaurant, then an early night and an early start. She might even make the noon train if she put a spurt on.

It took her almost an hour to shower and change because she felt no need to rush considering. At seven-thirty, she sat down on the bed again and picked up the phone to get an outside line, dialling the Medfield number with a delicious curling of anticipation.

Half an hour later she tried again, still without response. So perhaps he had taken himself out to dinner again, she told herself, and knew she didn't believe it. It had been his suggestion that she came down here overnight. And why? So that he could have a last fling with Sharon. Or maybe not even his last. After all, it would be six weeks before he was in any position to even see the blonde-haired boutique owner again, much less climb into her bed.

She didn't go down to dinner, but kept on phoning at fifteen-minute intervals until finally giving up at nine. The night was long, dark and wrought with the pangs of both hunger and suspicion combined. By the time morning came she felt like a limp rag, but determined on one thing. Ross was going to admit the truth to her if she had to fetch Sharon herself in on the act. What happened after that, she had no idea as yet. Deep down, a small part of her still clung to the hope that she was wrong.

Shopping was a strain under the circumstances. She bought only what she needed to complete yesterday's outfits, then headed for the station and the noon train with a feeling that all her efforts might very well have been in vain.

In spite of everything she had to eat something, and lunch did at least get her through a good part of the journey north. Tucked into a corner of the first class carriage, she pretended to sleep a little afterwards, unwilling to be drawn into the conversation her solitary travelling companion was obviously looking for. She heard the woman get out at Derby, and soon afterwards fell into a real sleep, lulled by the motion of the train and her lack of it the night before.

The dream was so vivd it contained actual sound, not just in her mind but surely in her ears. It was several moments before she realised she was not asleep but lying wedged in a most uncomfortable position with her legs trapped by the opposite seat section which appeared to have fallen on them. There was a lot of smoke, and the roof of the compartment seemed to have cracked—or concertinaed together might be a more appropriate word. In fact, the whole compartment looked distinctly smaller than before, the doors and windows buckled, the latter smashed into jagged ends. Her coat, falling from the rack above under the impact, had protected her from the flying glass. Looking down it she could see thousands of pieces glinting up at her in the rays of the westering winter sun.

Impact. Closing her eyes again, she tried to remember, but it was all mixed up with her dream. Ross had been there and they had been shouting at one another, then she had screamed and he had reached out and pushed her hard back into her seat. The shouting was still going on: a lot of different voices, though, coming from both inside and outside the train. Somebody else was screaming, sounding more hysterical than agonised. Kerry was aware of no pain herself. Her legs simply felt numb from the knees down. Somewhere she recalled reading that this was a bad sign, but of what she couldn't decide. Her mind felt free and floating, almost detached from her body altogether. She was glad her suitcases had seen fit to land away from her; they hadn't even burst open. That was what came of buying good ones to start with. Andrew had always insisted that leather stood the test of time far better than any man-made substitute.

Somebody or something was wrenching at the outer door, prizing loose the jammed metal. The smoke was getting thicker, making her cough. A voice said, 'Hang on, love, we'll soon have you out of there,' but she couldn't summon the will to care. Breathing was becoming more difficult by the minute; there seemed to be some kind of fumes mingled with the smoke. If she could only . . .

She came to again in the ambulance racing along with siren blaring, and for a moment wondered who was so ill. There was a mask over her face and cold, funny-tasting air coming through it into her nose and mouth. She put up a hand and weakly tried to push the thing away, only to have it grasped and held gently down again.

'You're suffering from smoke inhalation,' the young, uniformed man said clearly. 'The oxygen will help clear it out. We'll be there soon.'

Where? she wondered. Home? Her sense jerked back to life for a moment. Ross! What about Ross? Had anyone told him what had happened?

It was like being back in the dream again for a long time after that. Vaguely, she was aware of being taken from the ambulance and wheeled along a long corridor with lights at regular intervals down the middle of the ceiling. There was a lift, another corridor just like the first, and then at long last a bed and kind hands helping her out of her clothing. For the first time she had feeling in her legs; not pain exactly, more a dull ache. She was given something to drink, and felt the prick of a needle. Gradually everything faded away.

This time there was shaded electric lighting on when she awoke. She was lying semi-propped against a couple of pillows, arms relaxed along each side of her almost as if they didn't belong. Ross was sitting at the side of the bed, a hand covering one of hers. He looked drawn, as if he hadn't slept for a long time.

'Hi,' he said softly. 'How do you feel now?'

'Parched,' she said. 'My tongue is so dry it's sticking to the roof of my mouth!'

He let go of her hand to stand up and pour what looked like orange juice into a glass. 'Shall I hold it for you?' he asked.

'Oh, no, I'm fine.' She took it from him gratefully and drank, feeling new life flowing into her along with the liquid. 'That's nectar!' She looked at him for a long moment, trying to read the strong features. 'You look awfully tired,' she said at last. 'How long have you been here?'

'A couple of hours. I got the call about four-thirty. It's gone eight now.' His voice roughened. 'All I was told was that you'd been taken to hospital after being involved in the derailment. I'd heard the news flash on local radio, but I thought you were taking the three-fifty.'

'Last-minute change of plan.' Her mind shied away from the reason for it. 'Poor Ross, it mush have been quite a shock.'

'Shock?' He sounded as if he were trying the word out for size. 'Yes, I suppose you could call it that.' His gaze went over her face, detail by detail, the expression in his eyes bringing her heart pounding into her throat. 'All I remember is thinking that if you died I'd lost everything worth living for. I love you, Kerry. I never realised just what that word meant until this afternoon.'

'Ross.' Her voice was thick, her hand going out to him

gropingly. 'Oh, Ross, you don't know how I've longed to hear you say that! You never did before—not in that sense.'

He smiled a little, taking the hand and squeezing it tightly. 'If it comes to that, neither did you. Just sexual, you said the other night.'

'I was just trying to school myself to accept it that way.' Her eyes had misted. 'I do love you, Ross. I think I always have—even when I hated you so much. I wanted you to notice me, to stop treating me like a schoolgirl. When you went away it was like the end of the world.'

He shook his head gently. 'You had a schoolgirl crush, that's all. Don't start building on something that wasn't there. We saw one another properly for the first time the day I came home. Only other things got in the way.'

'Sinclairs,' she murmured, and saw his lips twist.

'To hell with Sinclairs. I'd have burned it down myself if it would have saved you for me!'

Kerry glanced down at the mound made by her legs, hardly daring to try moving them. 'Ross, I—I don't have any real injuries, do I?'

'Only bruising and a few minor cuts, thank God. Apparently you were trapped by the seat falling on them, but the padding saved you. They had to rip out half the compartment to get to you.'

'Was anyone else hurt?'

'Four, including the engine driver. No fatalities. If they catch the people responsible for putting that boulder on the line they want to put them away for life!'

She shuddered, remembering the screeching sound of the brakes penetrating her sleep, the suffocating smoke. Then Ross's lips were on hers and everything was all right again. She clung to him, wanting the strength of his arms about her for ever.

'I want to go home,' she said thickly when she could

speak again. 'Ross, please take me home.'

'I can't. Not until tomorrow. They want you in for overnight observation just to make sure.'

'But you're staying? You won't leave me here?'

'No, I won't leave you. I'll get a room in a local hotel for the night and come back first thing in the morning. Then we'll go home.'

A nurse came in then, crossing to the bed to take Kerry's wrist and start timing her pulse rate, her smile when she finished, reassuring.

'A little fast, but perhaps we can put that down to your fiancé. I'm afraid you'll have to leave now, Mr Sinclair. All being well, you'll be able to collect her in the morning after Dr Baker has seen her.'

'Right.' Undeterred by the nurse's presence, he bent and kissed Kerry on the lips. 'Goodnight, darling. I'll be back.'

'Nice,' commented the staff nurse appreciatively after he had gone out. 'I wish he was coming to take me home tomorrow!'

Kerry made some suitably light rejoinder with an effort. Depression had swamped her again. Ross said he loved her and she believed him, but it didn't alter the fact that he had not been at home last night. Yet could she afford to let that suspicion spoil things now? True or not, it was up to her to make sure he had no need of other women from now on.

They reached Underwood in time for a late lunch prepared by a concerned and commiserating Mrs Payne.

'Would have been a real shame,' she said, 'if you'd had to put t' wedding back. Are you sure you're going to be fit to go straight off after?'

'Oh, yes,' Kerry assured her. 'I feel perfectly all right now. Just a bit stiff perhaps, but that will go. It isn't as if I'm going to be doing a lot of walking these next few days.' It wasn't until she caught Ross's faint grin that she realised what she had said. It made her stomach muscles knot. In less than twenty-four hours from now she would be Mrs Ross Sinclair, along with all that entailed. One more night to sleep alone and then the rest in his arms. She only hoped she could stop herself from caring about how many others had been there before her.

Fortunately she had done a lot of her packing over the weekend. There were only her new things, and the smoke had not penetrated the leather. The jade green suit she had bought to wear tomorrow was not supposed to be a lucky colour for weddings, but she had always felt it was the people who counted more than superstition. She and Ross were going to be happy. They loved one another, and that was all it took. But what about trust? a small voice in her mind asked. Could there ever be real happiness without that?

Ross made her sit down for tea at four, pouring it himself and bringing it across to her.

'You might not have been badly injured,' he said, 'but it has to have taken it out of you. I know it took it out of me, and I wasn't physically involved.'

'Just emotionally,' she said, savouring the word. She looked up at him standing in front of the fire, lean and dark; the very sight of him made her ache. 'Six whole weeks,' she murmured. 'I still can't believe it. We're actually going to be together for six weeks.'

'Night and day,' he agreed. 'You'll enjoy Rio, Kerry. I was there last year for Carnival.'

With whom? came the biting little thought. She pulled in her lower lip between her teeth, hating herself for her sheer inability to stop thinking that way. Ross was watching her expressionlessly; she hoped he hadn't guessed what was running through her mind. 'I suppose Christmas in itself is a Carnival out there,' she said quickly. 'It will be the first I've ever spent in a hot climate. It's going to seem strange without the turkey and plum pudding.'

'You'll be able to have that too if you want it. Cruise ships are a little world on their own. Ten to one they'll have a tree with all the trimmings, plus a special Christmas party for the big children as well as the small ones.'

She pulled a face at him. 'Does that mean me?'

'It means all of us.' He was smiling. 'Given the right circumstances we're all capable of reverting. Have you almost finished your packing?'

'Just about. Only shoes and sandals and I'm all set.'

'How many suitcases?'

'Three,' she confessed. 'Well, four if you count my handgrip.'

'You'd have done better with a cabin trunk. It's still not too late if you want to change. I could have one out here inside twenty minutes.'

'And ruin all my careful tissue folds? No, thanks.' A little diffidently, she added, 'How about you?'

'It's done. For the last time by me, I might add. In future I'll have a wife to take care of such details.'

Kerry laughed. 'It's almost like being married now. We share the same house, the same meals, see one another every day ...'

'Everything except occupy the same bed,' he finished. 'And tomorrow night we'll do that too. I made sure our cabin has a double.'

'Ross, you didn't! What will they have thought?'

'Exactly what I was thinking, I imagine. Here's a man who wants to feel his wife close to him in the night.'

Kerry closed her eyes for a moment, letting the longing wash over her. 'Ross, you're not going to regret being married to me, are you?' she asked on a low, uncertain note. 'I mean, once the newness wears off you won't get ... bored with me?'

'You're thinking about Margot again,' he said on a slightly harder note. 'How many times do I have to tell you the difference? I didn't love her—neither, if it comes to that, did she love me. We were two people with the same basic need. There was nothing more than that to hold us together. End of story.'

'I know. And I'm sorry.' She tried to find the words to express herself properly. 'It's knowing that you've slept in the same bed with her—that you've held *her* close in the night. There must have been some times when you came close to loving her, even if only at first.'

He came to her then, taking the half empty cup from her and replacing it on the tray, before sitting down at her side and turning her towards him. His face was serious.

'Kerry, will you get it through your head that there's no comparison between what I felt for Margot and what I feel for you. Okay, she was good fun and I enjoyed having her around for a while, but I never at any time tried to make out it might last because I knew it wouldn't. With you I know it will. Don't ask me how or why I know; I couldn't begin to tell you. You're just going to have to take my word for it.'

And trust him. That was what it all boiled down to. She put her fingers to his lips and forced a smile. 'I will, Ross. I really will.'

His kiss was gentle when she would almost have welcomed roughness. 'I'd intended taking you out dancing tonight,' he said. 'As that's obviously out, I think we'll have a fairly early dinner and get in a good night's sleep instead. Mrs Payne is going to leave everything ready before she goes. All we'll have to do is serve it up.'

'We could have candlelight to create the right mood,' Kerry said lightly, and drew a faint smile.

'It might create too much of a mood. Would you like some fresh tea?'

'Yes, but I'll get it,' she came back firmly. 'I'm not an invalid. Even the stiffness is gradually wearing off. I'll have to keep my legs covered for the first week or so, though. They're going to be black and blue.'

Ross looked down at them, long and slender, his hand reaching out to touch and soothe one of the longer abrasions down her shin. 'Thank God it was no worse. Bruises disappear eventually, even though they can hurt like hell at the time.' His movement was abrupt. 'I'll have more tea too.'

Mrs Payne left around six. Before she went she pressed a small, neatly wrapped package into Kerry's hands with a half embarrassed haste.

'Just a bit of something on account of you won't be getting many presents, it being a secret and all,' she said. 'It's from Billy and Sheila as well. We all put to.'

The 'bit of something' turned out to be the most exquisite little crystal vase, just right for a posy of flowers. Kerry exclaimed with pleasure. 'Oh, Mrs Payne, it's beautiful! Thank you.'

'It's not very big,' observed Mrs Payne judiciously, 'but I thought as how it might just go in that little alcove in t' drawing room. And it does go with your other stuff, doesn't it?'

'The Waterford? Oh yes. Actually I believe some of that came as wedding presents when Ross's parents were married themselves. Now I can add this to the collection, the old and the new.' On impulse Kerry leaned forward and kissed the lined cheek. 'Thank you again. Let me fetch Ross to see to it before you go.'

'There's time enough without getting him special.' Her face was all smiles. 'Now you enjoy yourselves on that boat, and come back all nice and brown. Mrs Sinclair you'll be then. It'll seem funny at first. Anyway, see you in six weeks.'

Six weeks from now, Kerry reflected when the woman had gone. Would she still be the same person, or would marriage have changed her whole outlook? Ross was such a strong personality, perhaps inevitably he would to a certain extent eclipse hers.

Because it was their last night as separate people, in the sense of names at least, she went to a lot of trouble in choosing what to wear, finally plumping for a short-skirted dress in red velour which had tiny buttons all the way down the front and a princess style waistline which made hers look little more than handspan. Downstairs again she went through to the kitchen to check on the gently simmering casserole, then found matches to light the candles through in the dining room.

She was on her way round via the hall when the telephone rang. Hoping it wasn't anything likely to spoil their plans for the evening, she lifted the receiver and gave the number in a distinctly discouraging tone.

'It's Bob Brown, miss,' announced a vaguely familiar voice over the wire. And then helpfully, 'Nightwatchman at t' Store. I was wondering like if Mr Sinclair would be coming tonight? Only he normally tells me beforehand, see, so's I don't have to keep alarm turned off longer than needs be. Like I said to him last night, can't be too careful after that job t' other week.'

'Last night?' Kerry felt dense, her mind refusing to sort out the meaning behind what he was saying. 'Mr Sinclair was in the Store last night?'

'That's right, miss. Came about eight same as usual and left about eleven. Works real hard, he does. Has a cup o' coffee out of my flask when I do t' ten o'clock round, and chats for a bit like.'

'How long has he been doing that?' It was almost sharp.

'Two or three nights a week, miss.' He sounded puzzled. 'It's made a bit of company having him in the place. Gets a bit lonely like at night.'

'Yes, I'm sure it must.' The blankness had given way to

tight-throated shame, husking her voice. 'No, he won't be coming in tonight, Mr Brown. We—— He's going away for a while.'

'Aye, well, I can settle down for a bit then.' He paused before tagging on kindly, 'And I hope as how you're feeling all right yourself after that train smash. We heard you'd not been hurt much like, but things like that can shake you up something rotten.'

Yes, she thought numbly, they certainly could. Aloud she said, 'No, I'm fine, thanks. It was nice of you to ask. I'll tell Mr Sinclair you called.'

'Tell Mr Sinclair *who* called?' asked Ross lightly from the foot of the stairs. 'I hope it wasn't someone expecting a call back, because they're going to have to wait six weeks.'

Kerry kept her tone level by sheer force of will, wanting to blurt out everything at once but recognising the possible advisibility of keeping a part of it to herself. 'It was the nightwatchman from the Store. He wanted to know if you'd be going in again tonight.'

'Damn, I forgot to tell him.' He glanced at her with a smile. 'Must have had other things on my mind.'

'He said you'd been going back to work in your office quite a lot these last few weeks,' she added in what she hoped were casual tones. 'I thought you seemed to have got pretty far with reorganisation plans, but couldn't you have done that equally well from home?'

'Too many distractions.' The shrug was wry. 'If I'd stayed around too much when you were here we'd have been bound to clash again some time, and I was following a policy of passive resistance.' A twinkle leapt in the grey eyes. 'It worked too, didn't it? I could almost feel the frustration in you when I stopped chasing you round the house.'

'You never chased me,' she returned in the same vein. 'You did the catching before I had chance to run!'

'That was policy too—at the time. I was still working out which way to handle you for the best.'

'The best what?'

'Results.' Laughing, Ross put an arm about her and guided her towards the drawing room. 'Come and have a drink. I like the dress, by the way. Wouldn't have thought red could look so good with your colour hair.'

Dinner was, as always when Mrs Payne had prepared it, delicious, but Kerry barely tasted a thing. Her conscience was troubling her, and she knew it would not be an easily forgotten reason. If Ross noted any element of strain in her he failed to comment on it. In all probability he put it down to a combination of after-effects from the accident and pre-wedding nerves. He kept the conversation easy, barely touching on personal matters at all; they had a whole lifetime ahead of them for those.

They were back in the sitting room with coffee and brandy before Kerry finally bowed her head to the inevitable. She had to make the confession before she could put it out of her mind. The lights were blessedly low, the soft music an antidote to anger. Not that she really anticipated anger. Resigned exasperation might be closer.

She said it all of a piece, quickly, before she could change her mind. 'You know, I believed you were seeing Sharon West all these weeks. I still half believed it even after you denied it.'

He was lying back in the sofa, forearms crossed to support the nape of his neck, features semi-obscured in the flickering firelight. 'I know,' he said without particular inflection. 'I wondered how long it would take Bob Brown's little piece to make you admit it.'

She was silent for a long moment looking at him, trying to guess what he might be thinking. 'It didn't bother you?' she ventured at last.

'It bothered me.' The statement was matter-of-fact. 'I

had to let you find out your own way.'

'Supposing I never had?'

'I guess you'd have just gone on thinking what you were thinking. I told you once it wasn't true, I wasn't going to tell you again.' He looked at her then, turning his face from the firelight so that his expression was even more difficult to assess. 'There's a world of difference between lying and evading disclosures. I didn't tell you about Margot because one, it was over before I met you again, and two, I knew you wouldn't be able to take it.'

She sighed. 'You haven't heard the worst of it yet. I rang you on Wednesday night from the hotel.'

'I thought you were going to a show?'

'It was too late to bother by the time I got in.'

'If I'd known I'd have stayed at home.' The smile was faint. 'I'm distracted when you're here and restless when you're not.'

'I'm sorry,' she said.

'For what? Not trusting me?'

'I will in future.'

Ross shook his head. 'It's going to take time. I don't blame you. I haven't presented a particularly worthy image. I'd have used any trick in the book, or out of it, to stop you marrying your producer friend—and believe me, Sinclairs wasn't the driving force behind me that night!'

'You gave that impression.'

'Of course I gave that impression. I didn't think the hold I had on you was enough without it.'

'Little did you know.' Her voice caught. 'Oh, Ross, I do love you!'

He reached for her, turning her across him so that her head lay in the crook of his arm as he kissed her long and lingeringly. She responded without restraint, feeling him harden slowly into passion.

He had opened her dress down to her waist, his hand

moving with exquisite sensitivity of touch over her breast, starting the glow down deep. When he began unfastening the lower buttons she made no move to stop him, no longer caring about waiting—no longer caring about anything beyond what was happening right here and now.

It was Ross himself who stopped, the effort obvious. 'No,' he said roughly. 'We've come this far, we'll go the distance.' He pulled the dress around her again and sat her upright, pressing a swift kiss on her stiff lips. 'Best place for you is bed, out of temptation's way. We'll have all the time in the world tomorrow night.'

Kerry allowed herself to be put on her feet and have the buttons fastened. She hardly knew what to say to him. He was doing this because he thought it was what she wanted, but she didn't. Or did she? A moment or two ago there had been no doubt in her mind. She had wanted him all the way. Now . . .

'Cheer up,' he said on a deliberately light note. 'It didn't happen. You'll have that ring on your finger when it does. You go on up—the bride should get a good night's sleep. I'll clear away down here.'

Kerry went with uncertainty clouding her mind, aware of having failed him in some way. Yet she had done everything but actually say the words.

An hour later, lying in bed, it finally came to her that hearing her say it was possibly the one thing he had needed to be certain of her lack of regrets. She had said 'I love you, Ross' which to her meant so much; she had never once said 'I want you, Ross' which to him meant so much more.

He had come up about twenty-five minutes ago; she had heard him on the stairs. She lay there thinking about him, remembering the night he had come here to this room and waited for her to emerge from the bath, the sight of him lying here on this same bed, the feel of his hands and lips on her skin and the aching hunger he had aroused. That same hunger was in her now; born of her own desire, not his. She felt suddenly and joyously happy, knowing at last what she had to do.

The new negligés were packed away. She didn't bother getting one out but slipped on the same cotton wrap she had worn that night in the study. The landing was in darkness. She felt her way along it without switching on a light, passing the head of the stairs to the door of his room and opening it softly.

Ross was in bed lying on his back, but he wasn't asleep. He came up on one elbow as Kerry slipped into the room, the moonlight streaming through the window behind him silvering his hair.

'There's something I forgot to tell you downstairs,' she said. She let the wrap fall to the floor, seeing his face slowly change with a sense of gladness that she could put that look there. Emotion husked her voice. 'I want you, Ross. Not tomorrow night. Now.'

Mouth curving, he lifted the covers. 'Tomorrow night too, I hope.'

A long time afterwards, lying pliant and content in his arms, she began to smile.

'Anyway,' she said, 'I might be seasick!'

The Mills & Boon Rose is the Rose of Romance

Every month there are ten new titles to choose from – ten new stories about people falling in love, people you want to read about, people in exciting, far away places. Choose Mills & Boon. It's your way of relaxing.

February's titles are:

SUMMER OF THE WEEPING RAIN *by Yvonne Whittal*
Lisa had gone to the African veld for peace and quiet, but that seemed impossible with the tough and ruthless Adam Vandeleur around!

EDGE OF SPRING *by Helen Bianchin*
How could Karen convince Matt Lucas that she didn't want to have anything to do with him, when he refused to take no for an answer?

THE DEVIL DRIVES *by Jane Arbor*
Una was in despair when she learned that Zante Diomed had married her for one reason: revenge. How could she prove to him how wrong he was?

THE GIRL FROM THE SEA *by Anne Weale*
Armorel's trustee, the millionaire Sholto Ransome, was hardly a knight on a white horse – in fact as time went on she realised he was a cynical, cold-hearted rake . . .

SOMETHING LESS THAN LOVE *by Daphne Clair*
Vanessa's husband Thad had been badly injured in a car smash. But he was recovering now, so why was he so bitter and cruel in his attitude towards her?

THE DIVIDING LINE *by Kay Thorpe*
When the family business was left equally between Kerry and her stepbrother Ross, the answer seemed to be for them to marry – but how could they, when they didn't even like each other?

AUTUMN SONG *by Margaret Pargeter*
To help her journalist brother, Tara had gone to a tiny Greek island to get a story. But there she fell foul of the owner of the island – the millionaire Damon Voulgaris . . .

SNOW BRIDE *by Margery Hilton*
It appeared that Jarret Earle had had reasons of his own for wanting Lissa as his wife – but alas, love was the very least of them . . .

SENSATION *by Charlotte Lamb*
Helen's husband Drew had kept studiously out of her way for six years, but suddenly he was always there, disturbing, overbearing, and – what?

WEST OF THE WAMINDA *by Kerry Allyne*
Ashley Beaumont was resigned to selling the family sheep station – but if only it hadn't had to be sold to that infuriating, bullying Dane Carmichael!

If you have difficulty in obtaining any of these books from your local paperback retailer, write to:

Mills & Boon Reader Service
P.O. Box 236, Thornton Road, Croydon, Surrey CR9 3RU

The Mills & Boon Rose is the Rose of Romance

Look for the Mills & Boon Rose next month

THE MATING SEASON *by Janet Dailey*
When Jonni Starr got engaged, she thought she ought to go back to tell her parents. So back she went, and promptly fell in love with another man . . .

LOVE IS THE HONEY *by Violet Winspear*
Iris agreed that it was time she found out what life was like outside of her convent. So she went to work for the overwhelming Zonar Mavrakis – and found out with a vengeance!

SPIRIT OF ATLANTIS *by Anne Mather*
After the shock of her father's death, Julie was having a restful holiday in Canada. Restful? Not with the disturbing Dan Prescott around!

THE GOLDEN PUMA *by Margaret Way*
The abrasive David Hungerford thought that Catherine ought to leave her father to make a life of her own. But what life was there, without David – who wasn't interested in her in that way?

MAN OF ICE *by Rachel Lindsay*
Happy to accept a job with the kindly Miss Bateman, Abby found that she had brought on herself the contempt and suspicion of her employer's dour nephew Giles Farrow.

HOTEL JACARANDAS *by Katrina Britt*
Julie's sadness over her parents' divorce was nothing compared to her heartbreak when she fell in love with Felipe de Torres y Aquiliño – who didn't want her . . .

THE FIRST OFFICER *by Anne Weale*
Four years' separation had not lessened Katy's love for her husband. But Charles had been disillusioned by her once – had she reason to suppose she had any attraction for him now?

NIGHT MUSIC *by Charlotte Lamb*
'I bought you, and what I buy stays bought, even if it proves to be worthless,' Steve Crawford told Lisa. Would she be able to change his opinion of her?

DANGEROUS MARRIAGE *by Mary Wibberley*
Shelley knew nothing about the overbearing and mysterious Vargen Gilev except that she loved him – and he did not love her . . .

YOURS WITH LOVE *by Mary Burchell*
Virginia had fallen in love with Jason Kent as a result of playing 'the other woman' in a plot to get rid of Jason's wife. But how could Virginia go on caring about a man as selfish as he was?

Available March 1980

If you have difficulty in obtaining any of these books from your local paperback retailer, write to:

Mills & Boon Reader Service
P.O. Box 236, Thornton Road, Croydon, Surrey, CR9 3RU

The very best of Mills & Boon romances, brought back for those of you who missed reading them when they were first published.

in
February
we bring back the following four great romantic titles.

THE CASTLE IN THE TREES
by Rachel Lindsay
The very name of the Castle in the Trees fascinated Stephanie, and the reality was even more intriguing than she had imagined. But there was mystery there too. Why did Miguel and Carlos de Maroc hate each other? Stephanie found out at last, but only at the cost of losing her heart.

ISLAND OF PEARLS
by Margaret Rome
Many English girls go to Majorca for their holiday in the secret hope of meeting romance. Hazel Brown went there and found a husband. But she was not as romantically lucky as she appeared to be – for Hazel's was a husband with a difference . . .

THE SHROUDED WEB
by Anne Mather
For several very good reasons Justina wished to keep the news of her husband's death from her frail, elderly aunt. Then she heard of the Englishman Dominic Hallam, who was in hospital suffering from amnesia, and the germ of an idea came into her mind . . .

DEVIL IN A SILVER ROOM
by Violet Winspear
Margo Jones had once loved Michel, so when he died she found herself going to look after his small son in the French chateau of Satancourt. There Margo met Paul Cassilis, Michel's inscrutable brother, to whom women were just playthings, but in "Miss Jones" was to find one woman who was determined not to be.

Doctor Nurse Romances

and February's
stories of romantic relationships behind the scenes
of modern medical life are:

NURSE ON WARD NINE
by Lisa Cooper

It was a wrench for Claire Melville to leave home – and Martin – to nurse at the Princess Beatrice Hospital, and on Ward Nine she encountered hazards she had never expected – not least that cold-eyed, moody Doctor Andrew MacFarlane!

SATURDAY'S CHILD
by Betty Neels

Saturday's child works hard for a living.... And so did Nurse Abigail Trent, plain and impoverished and without hope of finding a husband. Why did she have to fall in love with Professor Dominic van Wijkelen, who hated all women and Abigail in particular?

Order your copies today from your local paperback retailer

Masquerade
Historical Romances

MARIETTA
by Gina Veronese

Marietta was the richest woman in Florence – but when she fell in love with Filippo, poor but proud, she discovered that her wealth counted for nothing . . . . It could not recover his lost inheritance, or save them both from danger.

THE REBEL AND THE REDCOAT
by Jan Constant

Events of the Scottish uprising in 1745 apparently proved Anstey Frazer a murderess. Yet, on the long and gruelling journey south to her awesome trial, she found herself increasingly attracted to the Redcoat captain who was her captor . . . .

Look out for these titles in your local paperback shop from
8th February 1980

SAVE TIME, TROUBLE & MONEY!
By joining the exciting NEW...

WITH all these EXCLUSIVE BENEFITS for every member

NOTHING TO PAY! MEMBERSHIP IS FREE TO REGULAR READERS!

IMAGINE the *pleasure* and *security* of having ALL your favourite *Mills & Boon* romantic fiction delivered right to *your* home, absolutely POST FREE... straight off the press! No waiting! No more disappointments! All this PLUS all the latest news of *new books* and *top-selling authors* in your own monthly MAGAZINE... PLUS *regular* big CASH SAVINGS... PLUS lots of wonderful strictly-limited, *members-only* SPECIAL OFFERS! All these exclusive benefits can be *yours* – right NOW – simply by joining the exciting NEW *Mills & Boon* ROMANCE CLUB. Complete and post the coupon below for FREE full-colour leaflet. It costs nothing. HURRY!

No obligation to join unless you wish!

FREE CLUB MAGAZINE Packed with advance news of latest titles and authors

Exciting offers of **FREE BOOKS** For club members ONLY

Lots of fabulous **BARGAIN OFFERS** –many at **BIG CASH SAVINGS**

FREE FULL-COLOUR LEAFLET!

CUT OUT

CUT-OUT COUPON BELOW AND POST IT TODAY!

To: MILLS & BOON READER SERVICE, P.O. Box No 236, Thornton Road, Croydon, Surrey CR9 3RU, England.

WITHOUT OBLIGATION to join, please send me FREE details of the exciting NEW **Mills & Boon** ROMANCE CLUB and of all the exclusive benefits of membership.

Please write in BLOCK LETTERS below

NAME (Mrs/Miss) ....

ADDRESS ....

CITY/TOWN ....

COUNTY/COUNTRY .... POST/ZIP CODE ....

S. African & Rhodesian readers write to:
P.O. BOX 11190, JOHANNESBURG, 2000. S. AFRICA